The Convention

Tales from a Revolution: Massachusetts

**Also by Lars D. H. Hedbor,
available from Brief Candle Press:**

The Prize: Tales From a Revolution - Vermont
The Light: Tales From a Revolution - New-Jersey
The Smoke: Tales From a Revolution - New-York
The Declaration: Tales From a Revolution - South-Carolina
The Break: Tales From a Revolution - Nova-Scotia
The Wind: Tales From a Revolution - West-Florida
The Darkness: Tales From a Revolution - Maine
The Path: Tales From a Revolution - Rhode-Island
The Freedman: Tales From a Revolution - North-Carolina
The Tree: Tales From a Revolution - New-Hampshire
The Mine: Tales From a Revolution - Connecticut
The Siege: Tales From a Revolution - Virginia
The Will: Tales From a Revolution - Pennsylvania

The Convention

Lars D. H. Hedbor

Brief Candle Press

Copyright ©2021 Lars D. H. Hedbor

This is a work of historical fiction. Apart from the well-known actual people, events, and locales that figure in the narrative, all names, places, and incidents are products of the author's imagination or are used fictitiously.

ALL RIGHTS RESERVED. This book contains material protected under the International and Federal Copyright Laws and Treaties. No part of this book may be reproduced or transmitted in any form or any means, electronic or mechanical, including photocopying, recording, or by any information storage and retrieval system without specific written permission from the publisher.

Cover and book design: Brief Candle Press.
Cover image based on "The Hut Camp on the Dyckman Farm," John Ward Dunsmore, 1915. Courtesy of the New York Public Library.
Map reproduction courtesy of Library of Congress, Geography and Map Division.
Fonts: Allegheney, Doves Type, and IM FELL English.

First Brief Candle Press edition published 2021.
www.briefcandlepress.com

ISBN: 978-1-942319-61-0

Dedication

*for Jenn,
with gratitude
for her patience*

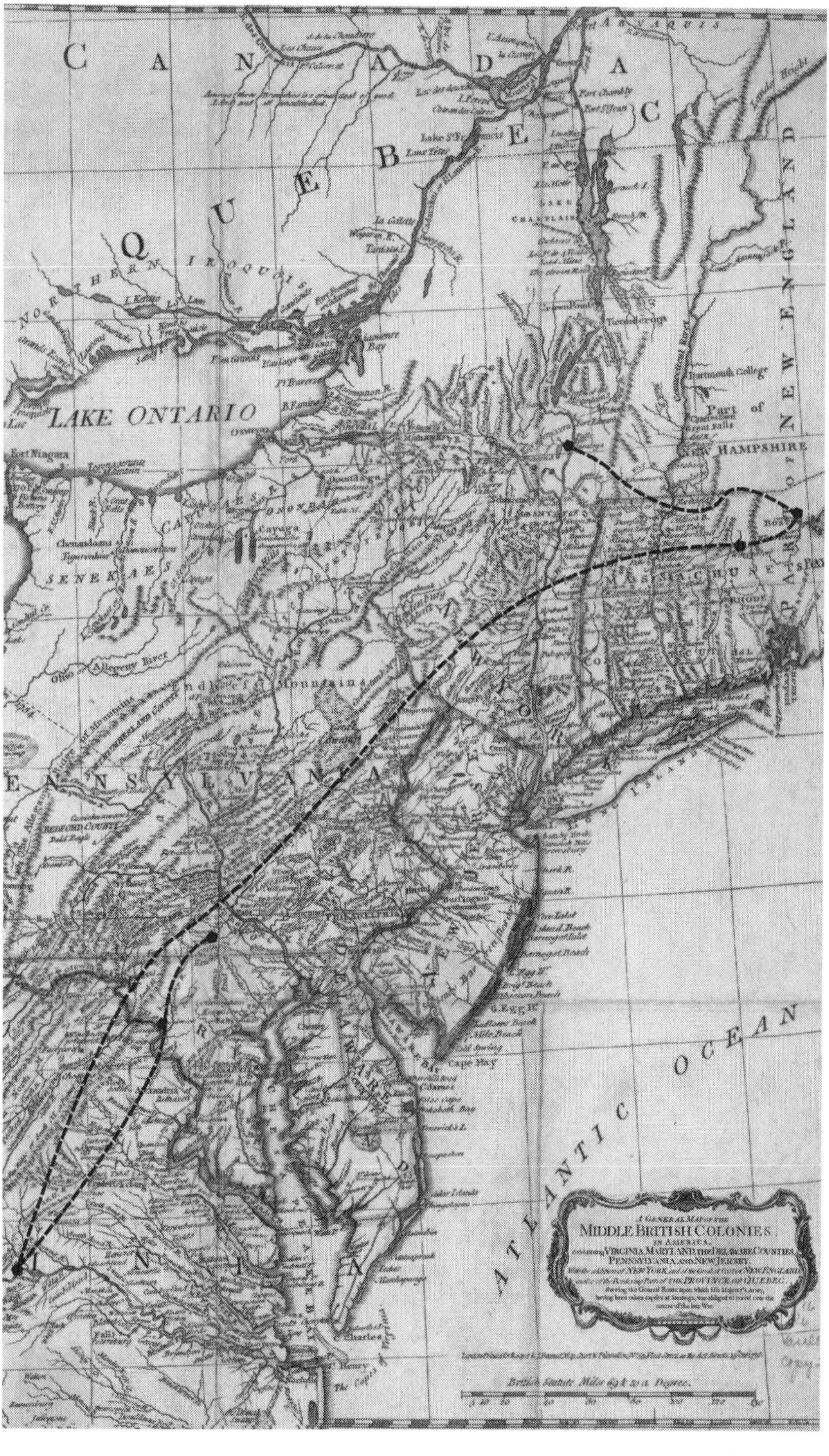

A GENERAL MAP OF THE
MIDDLE BRITISH COLONIES,
IN AMERICA,
VIRGINIA, MARYLAND, the DELAWARE COUNTIES,
PENNSYLVANIA and NEW JERSEY.
NEW YORK
PROVINCE of QUEBEC
British Statute Miles 69½ to a Degree.
CANADA
QUEBEC
LAKE ONTARIO
Part of
NEW HAMPSHIRE
NEW ENGLAND
ATLANTIC OCEAN
Endless Mountains
Allegeny River
Ticonderoga
Dartmouth College
Cape May
Cayuga

Chapter I

Arthur Leary bent and picked another stone out of the mud where the farmer's plow had revealed it, tossing it onto the sledge that he pulled behind himself. Where the rocks all came from, he could not imagine, as it seemed impossible that there could be any left. The tidy rock walls bounding the field in which he labored seemed to bear witness to the removal of what must have been tons of stone from just this section of muddy soil.

Thinking of the weight of the stone in the walls already only made the sledge seem heavier as he yanked it into motion again. Noting his progress by his position relative to the tree that stood on the far side of the boundary, he decided it was time to empty the sledge again before continuing to add to the load upon it.

He dragged the sledge to the spot at the edge of the field where the products of his prior passes were already roughly piled, and dropped its rope before trudging back to start tossing rocks off the mud-spattered platform. The mindless, repetitive motions of lifting, swinging, and releasing each stone in turn gave him plenty of time to reflect on just how he'd come to be an ordinary laborer on a New-England farm.

Answering the call of His Majesty's army recruiter had seemed sensible enough. As the third son of a smallholder in a windswept part of England near to the old Scottish frontier, he stood to inherit nothing but his name and a few years of education, if that. In contrast, service in the army offered him steady employment and the possibility of returning home covered in glory for acts of heroism and daring.

The months following his enlistment had been a blur of learning drill and becoming accustomed to the quirks of the reliable old musket they'd issued him. But he kept up with the pace of firing, clearing, and making ready that his superiors demanded of him — perhaps too well. One evening, he was pulled aside by his sergeant, a man whose face was marked by the pox, and whose teeth gave ample evidence of being ready for the dentist's extractor.

"The lieutenant says you're to be appointed to the rank of corporal. Mostly, it just means that the officers will hold you responsible for not only you own conduct, but that of your men, as well. On the bright side, you'll be paid half again a private's wage, so it's not all bad."

Arthur swallowed hard and nodded.

The extra pay did a man little good if there was nowhere to spend it in the village but Missus Chester's house of ill repute, but he already knew better than to decline what small honors might come his way. Even if they were as dubious as this one, they were still a rarity.

One day, the order had come to ship out to America. America! He'd groaned when he'd heard the long-expected word. "What have they which is worth fighting over?" he asked his sergeant.

The man grunted noncommittally. "Doesn't matter, Leary. The lieutenant says we're going, and that's the final word. It doesn't do to start questioning the orders you're given this early in your career." He grinned, showing his crooked and stained teeth. "You'll have plenty of time to do that when the cannon balls start flying. Muster your men, and see that they are ready for transport."

Then came – he begged the Author of All to forgive him the thought – the most Godforsaken eleven weeks of his entire life, mostly fit only to be forgotten as quickly as possible.

There was day after day of sheer terror at sea, as nothing remained in one place for more than a minute, including the tenuous bit of dry space upon which one stood, and one's stomach. The laughing sailors who climbed the rope rigging of the ship as though it were a fine staircase assured him that the passage was hardly any worse than usual. If that were true, Arthur hoped to never experience a truly bad passage.

As the convoy approached Boston, a passing Royal Navy patrol informed them that the city had fallen to the rebels, so they all instead bent their path northward, to Québec.

All but one, that was. One of the merchant transports had absconded with a hold full of good powder and other items useful to the rebel forces, betraying his ship to the American cause.

Regardless of the unexpectedly altered destination and various setbacks, Arthur had gratefully disembarked at the city of Québec, and thought that he might die a happy man if he never tasted fish again.

In Québec, his squad had set up their crisp, white tents, content to follow the labor with a relative feast of bread, small beer, and even a small portion of salt pork. Having a table to sit at where one didn't regularly have to dart out a hand to recapture a knife set into motion by the sea was enough to make even this simple repast taste finer than he could remember the best meal in his mother's kitchen ever tasting.

The Convention

After a few weeks' recovery from their ordeal at sea, they engaged in some cheerful skirmishes against the American forces that had been foolhardy enough to remain in the province after their disastrous attempt at Québec City in the dead of the winter prior.

The Americans there having been reduced sufficiently for local forces to deal with, the departure of the army Arthur was attached to from Québec City was an orderly enough affair, but it quickly turned sour in his estimation. They were directed to load their chests not onto wagons, as he had expected, but onto low, flat-bottomed boats, pulled up in a long row along the shoreline.

The sergeant motioned his men to come within earshot, and then spoke in a clear, loud voice. "We're to row up the river, to where it opens into a lake. There, we will follow our guides toward the fort that the enemy seized from us last year through treachery, and we will restore it to Crown control, by whatever means necessary. After that..."

His voice trailed off and he raised one eyebrow significantly before continuing. "After that, we will be given such further commands as our officers see fit to share with us."

Arthur scoffed inwardly. Was this another command given by officers who would never have to labor at an oar themselves, and given without regard for what price it would exact of those who must answer to it?

He had reason to ask that question again when they arrived within sight of Fort Ticonderoga. The stronghold towered over the lake atop a headland that Arthur could just see past the ships carrying the officers and supplies. It looked impregnable even to his unpracticed eye.

He flinched as the first gout of flame erupted from the cannon atop the fort – the Americans' greeting to the British forces. While his squad was directed to beach its boat, the men within the fort continued firing cannon in their direction at a desultory rate, apparently more for range and harassment than for effect . . . so far.

Setting up their tents, weary from rowing, the men in Arthur's unit were not much inclined to converse beyond the necessary directions to finish the task before them and prepare a meal before falling into a sleep only slightly disrupted by the bark and boom of cannon.

The next morning, the lieutenant himself had come around, and after summarizing the defenses, he revealed that a scouting party had found a position that would negate all the advantages of the Americans' position within the fort . . . at the top of a neighboring mountain.

The officer smiled, his mouth tight and grim. "Naturally, the rebels will be sensible of the danger should they discern what we mean to do. Furthermore, there is no road, so we shall have to cut one out of the forest that stands between us and the peak."

He surveyed his men. "You have been selected to perform this task, and I trust that you will discharge your duties with all possible dispatch. I will turn you over to the capable hands of Lieutenant Twiss of the engineering company, and you will follow his orders exactly."

The following morning, after a day and night of incredible labor, they'd succeeded in bringing a pair of twelve-pounders up to the peak. Arthur stared in satisfaction down into the fort that had seemed so imposing from the surface of the lake. While they'd still been making ready to rain iron down onto the unsuspecting rebel forces, the enemy had spotted the emplacement, or been informed of it by their scouts, though, and the Americans had fled into the New-Hampshire Grants.

Fort Ticonderoga once again flew the pennant of Britain, and although the enemy had escaped capture, the way was clear for whatever the generals might have planned next.

That turned out to be a hard march, then a set battle with the American forces. They'd found the enemy dug into a spot that overlooked a wide, open field, and the general had ordered an attack.

Although the Americans yielded the ground before the end of the day, it had cost the lives of Arthur's sergeant and many scores of other men.

The mingled scents of gunpowder, the stink of terrified men, and the sharp, metallic tang of blood – blood everywhere he turned – would forever dominate Arthur's memory of the battle.

Through it all, he'd somehow clung to the naïve belief that they would take the day, and that a victory this momentous would be marked by toasts to the King and tables groaning with a feast.

Instead, he'd observed the battle's conclusion by closing his sergeant's lifeless eyes and helping to dig graves all through the following day.

The accursed rebels had focused their fire on British officers, and the number of gentlemen Arthur helped carry off the field and lay to rest in this blood-soaked land was more than he could keep count of.

Alongside his sergeant, Arthur counted the broken corpses of fully a third of his own little squad, and another number had disappeared – though whether they were lying undiscovered somewhere on the tall grass, or had deserted, he could scarcely guess.

The end of the affair, when it came, was relatively swift. After those remaining fit to fight had closed on the Americans again, Arthur had endured another long day of desperate and hot fighting on the field of battle. The skirmishes sent what remained of his squad scurrying this way and that across the landscape, to stumble on fallen Englishmen and field hummocks alike.

All of their striving came to naught upon the arrival of an American madman in gleaming epaulets, who rode his horse in a frenzy between the lines, seeming to have no concern whatever for his personal safety. As taken aback as the British line was at his appearance, the rebels were heartened, and pressed their attack forward, eventually causing the men around Arthur to break ranks and run.

As far as Arthur was concerned, the ceremony of surrender, which ought to have been a humiliation, was in truth a relief. The few remaining men of his squad looked sharp and professional, in new uniforms issued out of the supply train for the occasion. The Americans assembled before them were comparatively slovenly in appearance, with hardly anything like a consistent uniform.

He had to grudgingly admit that they were turned out in good order, though, and they maintained their formation well enough as they watched their vanquished foes pass in review before them, disarmed, as they'd stacked their weapons just before coming into the ceremony.

Arthur was not sad to see his cantankerous old musket pass into American control, and he half-hoped that the barrel would

The Convention

finally explode in the hands of its new American owner.

However, the music playing as they passed in review made Arthur grit his teeth. The cheeky, jeering little tune "Yankee Doodle" had long since surpassed being merely an inspiration to the Americans, and had transformed into a taunt against their foe.

He was mildly surprised when his unit had returned with the others to standing at attention in their formation, to see that when General Burgoyne handed his sword over to the American general — Gates, he thought the man's name was — the enemy officer examined it closely and then handed it back. It was a civilized gesture of respect that he hardly thought the Americans capable of.

The lieutenant had explained the terms of surrender before the army had set out for the ceremony. General Burgoyne had secured many important concessions from the Americans, including the most important: they would march out to Boston, and board ships bound for home, never to return to this fight.

Arthur would be glad enough to quit America and to forsake it forever. Still, he did have to admit, now that summer had given way to fall, the countryside was altogether lovely. Beyond the placid river flowing by, the hills were a riotous mass of color, including some hues that he would have sworn could not be produced by nature. He became less enamored of the countryside, though, on having to make his way through it.

The march to Cambridge, overlooking Boston, was arduous and painful. The weather turned quickly from gentle autumn to bitter winter, and in the storms, some uncounted number more of their ranks had disappeared — whether fallen unnoticed at the wayside, or slipped away in desertion, it was impossible to say.

Yet more men fell to disease and misfortune in the camps at night, including some of their German jägers who froze to death after being denied shelter by New-Englanders who seemed to hold the Germans in special contempt for their role in the war. Even as Arthur's pitiful squad huddled for warmth in a barn, the jägers were obliged to huddle in unheated tents, or completely out of doors.

Arthur didn't quite understand it — but then, there was a lot about the New-Englanders that confounded him.

When the defeated army finally arrived at Cambridge, instead of being offered proper barracks in which they could wait to embark from Boston, they were shown to a wretched and nearly collapsed set of hovels, which someone had told him were left over from Washington's siege of Boston.

Despite the vindictive American guards and a persistent lack of supplies — and more importantly, of rations — the "Convention Army," as they'd come to call themselves, had put the camp into some semblance of order. They were held under the terms of the convention between Gentleman Johnny Burgoyne and the American General Gates, and that name stuck.

Rumors flew about the camp, giving hope to all that they might see home by springtime. Although the Boston port was largely closed by British blockade and the season's tides, they were to march to another port and embark any day.

Then the lieutenant had come into camp with news that dashed all hope. "Those rascals in their Congress! They've denied the general's request to put out from Rhode-Island, insisting that they will honor only the very letter of the convention." His lieutenant's face was red with the exertion of his anger, and Arthur was glad to not be its target. So he sat quietly and let the man rage on until he ran out of invective and excused himself to go and commiserate with the other officers.

A few weeks later, the lieutenant came bearing even worse news. "Not only will we not be permitted to embark at the more convenient port in Rhode-Island, but I should be most surprised if we are permitted to embark at all."

Arthur's eyebrows shot up, and he felt his stomach drop — ironically, the feeling not dissimilar to the sensation of being aboard a ship cresting a great wave. "On what basis could these rebel scum justify so completely breaking the convention?" He could hear the heat in his voice, but in his heart, he was past caring.

"As General Burgoyne has already declared the convention broke, and the Congress concluded that there were details of our conduct in surrender that did not conform to their satisfaction, they have claimed that they need not be bound by the terms of the convention. They say now that the terms of our surrender must be ratified by the Parliament as an accord between our government and their Congress."

"That selfsame Congress which our Parliament has steadfastly refused to recognize as speaking in place of Crown government on these shores?"

"Aye, you have smoked it exactly. The Congress has backed General Burgoyne into a corner, and left him with no possibility of escape. Though we might like to be exchanged for such prisoners as our armies may capture, the plain fact is that we here are so numerous that such an exchange may not be effected for some time to come."

While Arthur absorbed this news, his heartbeat roaring in his ears, the lieutenant added, in a tone of sad resignation, "It seems likely that we are to be the guests of these American colonies until this unhappy war is concluded."

With this dour prediction seeming to come true, and rations at the camp becoming shorter and shorter, when the lieutenant came around a few weeks later, his news piqued Arthur's interest extremely.

"Should you like to remove yourself from this camp, our hosts have offered up a chance to do so without raising any question of your loyalties or your adherence to the terms of our captivity."

"Say on," Arthur urged.

"I mean no slight against you or your men for your diligence in our encampment here, but if you wish, you may each offer yourselves up to labor at farms in the country around. It's harder duty than you have here in the barracks, but it's not without its compensations."

Arthur's brow furrowed deeply. "Why would they want us to labor on their fields?"

The lieutenant gave him a grim smile. "With so many of the young men of this country under arms to oppose His Majesty's forces, there are not enough left to do what is needed on the farms they leave behind. Only those too old to do such work, and those too young."

"And what are these 'compensations?'"

"A warm place to sleep, good food on the table . . . and you are not forbidden the cider-barrel, either, which is a nice relief when the sun is high."

That decision had been the easiest Arthur had made in all the time since he'd answered the recruiter's call. Even as his back ached over the load of stone, he was glad to have taken it, and grateful to have escaped the barracks.

Chapter 2

Just as he was unloading the last of this load, Mister Hillyard, the owner of the farm, emerged from his barn, where he'd been tending to his animals. Arthur glanced at the sun, judging it to be still short of noon, though it was already sufficiently high in the sky to bring a bead of sweat to his brow.

Hillyard drew close enough to call out, "Looks like the field's been productive of the stone this year, eh?"

It was the same witticism that he'd repeated every time he'd come to speak with Arthur since he'd put the British soldier to this menial, backbreaking task. The first time, it had been mildly amusing. The tenth time, less so.

"Aye, sir. You should get another course on the fence all around the field, at this rate."

"Pity you don't know stone dressing, much as you talk about the walls."

"Aye, sir, 'tis a pity. The best I could do for you would be to stack them up neatly, but without proper dressing, they'll likely just tumble down again. Back home, my Da hired a man who came around every summer. That fellow knew the art of it so well that he'd be done fixing what needed it before the end of day, most times. I followed him around one time, but my Da made me stay away after a stone chip caught me on the cheek."

Arthur pointed at an old scar on his face, and the farmer

nodded, obviously only half-following his story. "We'll cross that bridge when we come to it, then. It's not as if there won't be more stone to replace any that did come down, but 'tis a hassle, having to work it more than once."

The man nodded to himself once more, this time more briskly. "When you're done this field, come in and have your supper. Constance will have it ready by that time." He looked Arthur over, wrinkled his nose, and said, "You should probably avail yourself of the pond before you come in, though."

Arthur tilted his head in acknowledgment, but didn't say anything as he stooped to pick up the last rock from the sledge and move it over to the pile. When he looked up, Mister Hillyard was already going inside the house. He frowned and picked up the rope to bring the sledge back out to where he'd been working.

He knew that he shouldn't be irritated with the man — indeed, an invitation to come and eat with the family was more than he was due, and he had until now exclusively eaten in his quarters in the barn — but he couldn't help feeling a flash of anger at the fact that this peasant farmer thought him so low and grimy that he had to be *told* to bathe before coming into the house.

Just as he was building up a proper sense of righteous indignation, he lost his footing and went down face-first into the mud. He sprang up from the ground, cursing and spitting mud out of his mouth. But over his own ruckus, he heard the bubbling sound of laughter from behind him, and he whirled around.

Miss Hillyard stood at the stone wall, a large tin cup in one hand, and the other covering her mouth, though she could not contain the mirth that danced in her eyes. Seeing Arthur's shoulders slump, she called out quickly, "I am sorry for laughing, but I misdoubt that you could have contained yourself, either, had you seen it. Are you unhurt?"

Arthur looked down sourly at his hands, which had taken the brunt of his fall, but said, "Aye, I think so, other than my pride, which may never recover."

She held the cup up higher and added, "My father said that you looked heated from your labors, and I thought to bring you some switchel to cool you off."

Arthur mastered his frustration with a deep breath and replied, "That was most thoughtful of you, Miss Hillyard." He dropped the rope to the sledge and trudged over, suddenly keenly aware of the filth that encrusted not just his face and hands, but nearly every inch of his clothing.

She held the cup out to him, and he couldn't help but notice that her hand trembled ever so slightly. He accepted her offering, wondering if the oath that had escaped his lips had been so shocking to her ears, or if something else had her nerves high.

He gave her what he hoped was a grateful-looking smile and drank deeply from the cup.

Switchel had taken a little getting used to after he'd arrived on the farm, but there was no denying that under the heat of the day, the mixture of water, vinegar, and molasses was almost miraculously refreshing. He drained the cup and handed it back, his smile far broader now.

"You are too kind, Miss Hillyard, and I do not blame you in the slightest for laughing at what had to have been a ridiculous sight." A clump of mud fell from his brow just then, and he amended, "What still is a ridiculous sight."

She smiled back, and Arthur thought he saw a hint of

nervousness at the edge of her expression. He inclined his head respectfully. "I had best get back to work, so I can finish in time to accept your father's kind invitation to dinner."

"Oh, yes, of course. I hope you enjoy what I am preparing for us."

He smiled over his shoulder at her as he started back toward the sledge. "I am certain that I will."

For the rest of the afternoon, as he continued picking stones out of the soil, Arthur pondered how he had come to be at this particular farm, out of all of those whose proprietors had come to bid for the members of the Convention Army.

He remembered looking over the gaggle of farmers gathered at the American gaol that morning and first seeing Mister Hillyard. The man had been very particular on insisting that he be addressed as such, and Arthur suspected that it was because of the haughty demeanors of so many of the British troops, even the lowliest private soldiers.

The farmer had been notable primarily for the hat he'd worn that morning. Unlike so many of his neighbors, he had not chosen a cocked hat, practical though those could be for the sort of rainy day it was. Instead, Mister Hillyard wore a simple cap sewn of striped cloth. Somehow, it gave him a quiet dignity that the louder men lacked, flamboyant in their manner and in their felted hats, which were aggressively pinned and decorated with cockades, ribbons, and even feathers.

Mister Hillyard seemed to need none of that supposed finery to be taken seriously. When he advanced to the desk where the clark was taking down the details of the bids the Americans were placing for the various labor contracts on offer, Arthur had heard Mister Hillyard say gruffly, "Just need the one, no particular skills, though some experience of threshing would be welcome."

The clark looked at his hasty notes on the British soldiers who'd put their names on his roll, and said, "I think I've just the man for you. Before his service here, he was a farmer at home." Turning to the knot of prisoners, he called out, "Arthur Leary, please step forward and present yourself."

Doing his best to ignore the pitying looks that the men of his squad who'd joined him on the labor rolls shot him, Arthur had walked over to stand behind the clark, as the man indicated with a careless gesture of one hand.

Mister Hillyard looked Arthur over once, and nodded briskly. "He'll do. Any other bidders?"

"Nay, you'll be the first."

The farmer fished in his pocket and produced a small sheaf of bills, putting them on the small counter. "When will I know whether I've secured his services?"

The clark picked up the money and looked through it. "We will be going through the bids at the end of watch." He glanced over toward the sun, and added, "Perhaps two hours hence? Time enough to take your ease and have a drink or perhaps even sup."

He offered the bills back to the farmer. "Until then, you can keep this. We will only collect it once your bid has been accepted."

Mister Hillyard nodded again, folded the bills and put them back into his pocket. He turned away and said over his shoulder, "I will see you at the changing of the watch."

At the appointed time, the farmer had appeared, the clark collected his money, and just that simply, Arthur had new employment for the duration of his time in American custody. He wasn't even sure it was entirely legal under the terms of the convention, but he was happy enough to follow the farmer through the fence that had been thrown up around the barracks, and past the glowering guard at the gate.

He'd already said his farewells, gifting Jameson from his squad with the buckles from the pair of boots that had worn through on their travels. The man had surprised him on their journey from Saratoga by revealing that he had a wife in the van of the army.

More than that, Jameson had confessed that she was pregnant and that her labor had started, and Arthur had agreed to join him in asking the Almighty to permit them make it to some proper shelter before the babe was born.

Neither of their prayers did any good, though, as a vicious snowstorm halted the column on the road, where Arthur and several other men had been pressed into service by the midwife, to fashion a shelter for Jameson's wife as she delivered a baby boy in the howling wilderness.

Smiling slightly at the memory, Arthur expected that Jameson had immediately sold the buckles — a wife and a small son were no mean expense in the best of times — and that Miller similarly made some use of the duty jacket Arthur had left him other than wearing it, but he was glad enough to have been able to make the gesture.

After a long afternoon's walk, made longer and more arduous by the enforced inactivity of the past months, he was led by Mister Hillyard to the tidy farmhouse that the man shared with his wife and daughter.

The farmer had stopped at the door, and said, "You'll only

enter the house when you're invited. I've made up quarters for you in the barn, and according to the regulars who sold me your contract, you're expected to confine yourself to the boundaries of my property until you should be released from my service."

"Aye, Mister Hillyard. That was what I was given to understand when I signed up to be paroled out for labor."

"Good, I am happy to hear that there will be no misunderstandings, then. Unlike those Germans who eat morning, noon, and night, we eat at sunrise, and again at the end of the work day. I've no taste for strong drink, myself, so I haven't any of that around for you, either, but you'll grow to like the taste of switchel soon enough, I'll warrant."

He turned toward the barn, motioning for Arthur to follow him. Inside, he opened one of the stalls, which had apparently once held livestock, but was now swept clean and equipped with a pallet, a stool, and a small table. "I had Constance clean this space for you. Mind that you keep it tidy. You'll be warm enough in here, what with the animals and all. You'll get used to the smell before you know it."

In truth, Arthur had hardly noticed any particular odor from the animals, other than the warm musk of what smelled like goats. Now that he reflected on it, he should have expected some manure odor, and there was really scarcely any. His Da had always told him a clean barn was a healthy barn, though, and he was glad to see — and smell — that about this one.

"In my travels prior to coming here, I passed more than one night in barns that smelled far more strongly than this one," he said, truthfully. He didn't add that this one was probably even cleaner than his Da's.

Mister Hillyard smiled for the first time since Arthur had met him, and he said, "The cats keep mice and other pests out of here, and I don't expect that they'll bother you, but if they do, the door should keep them out."

"Oh, I don't mind a friendly cat." Arthur smiled, thinking that a cat or two might even make a warm companion on chilly nights.

Mister Hillyard shrugged and said, "Most of the ones we have are too skittish around people to let you more than glance them anyway." He motioned to Arthur's rucksack and added, "I'll let you get settled in and tell Constance to bring you your supper."

When he was alone, Arthur took his pack off, and set it down on the broad boards of the wooden floor. He permitted himself a small sigh of relief at having the weight off his shoulders, and sat on the sturdy little stool, loosening and removing his boots, taking a deep breath at having his feet free of their confines.

Miss Hillyard had appeared then, carrying a plate and a tin cup. Arthur's first impression of her was that she was quite petite, though no child — he guessed she was about his age — and pretty in a way that might not have caught his eye once upon a time, but which was quite pleasant to behold now.

She brought the food over to his table and set it before him. Speaking for the first time, she said, "Your supper, Mister Leary. We have no extra fork, but my father thought you might have your own, or at least a knife."

He smiled at her. "I thank you most kindly, Miss Hillyard. I'll make do just fine." He motioned about the stall. "And thank you, also, for your attention to my comfort in preparing this room for me."

She averted her eyes and said, "Oh, 'twas only a bit of sweeping. My father cannot abide a filthy barn, and so it was hardly any extra effort at all."

He inclined his head in acknowledgment. "Nonetheless, I am grateful. Have I any duties that you know of after dining?"

"Nay, we usually take our rest after dinner. Father does not like to spend money on lamps or candles to ward off the darkness, unless it is utterly necessary."

"Then I had best eat while I have light," Arthur said, smiling once more. "Thank you, again."

She ducked her head and left, stopping briefly at the door to say, "Sleep well, Mister Leary."

She was gone before Arthur could reply.

Chapter 3

When Arthur was finished unloading the last of the stones he'd pulled from the field, he went to the pond and washed his hands before going to his room and retrieving his second set of slops. He then returned to the pond and set the garment on the grass to change into after he bathed.

In the water, he scraped and wrung out his filthy clothes, glad that his sergeant had — so long ago, it seemed now! — ingrained in him the habit of maintaining his clothing as well as conditions permitted.

It was hard to tell, in the murky water of the pond, whether he'd gotten all of the stains out of his shirt and breeches, but he was confident that he had at least gotten the most egregious of the mud off of them.

He splashed water in his face to finish cleaning that, as well, and leaned back to rinse out whatever mud might still be in his hair. With long-practiced hands, he quickly drew the water out of the hair at the back of his head, folded it into a neat club, and secured it with the clean ribbon he'd put atop his clothes on the bank.

Rubbing his hand over his freshly scrubbed face, he wished he had a glass so that he might shave before presenting himself for supper . . . but that would need to wait for another opportunity.

He made his way out of the pond, and dressed, regretting for a moment that he no longer had his uniform, which he would have liked for the occasion of dining with the family.

However, he reflected that having a soldier in British uniform at their table might not go over well, and might even raise questions with any neighbor who happened by during the meal. His slops were not as tidy as his uniform, but they were serviceable.

His breeches might have been more appropriate for a dinner, but he no longer had the stockings to give a proper presentation of them, and it would be a day or more before the breeches were dry enough to wear anyway.

The loose trousers and shirt of his working clothes would hardly offend anyone at this table, in any event. Though Mister Hillyard might require formality in speaking to him, the farmer's manners did not seem to extend to putting on airs in his dress.

Satisfied he would be accepted in his current state, Arthur detoured to the barn to hang up his cleaned clothes and then went to the door of the house to present himself for supper.

The table was laid with the same sort of plain, but plentiful food to which he'd grown accustomed in the past weeks. However, it seemed to taste a little better, and have a more civilized air in general when served at a proper table, at which he was now seated in a real chair with a back.

Although the farm appeared to be moderately prosperous, Arthur was a little surprised at the lack of servants — Mister Hillyard's wife and daughter served the table themselves — and was even more surprised to see that the same tinware on which Miss Hillyard brought him his meals in the barn was what the entire family used.

At home, the family of a farm of this size would have been attended by at least a cook and a maid, and he didn't know if this was just one of the many differences between subjects of the King here and those in England itself, or if there were some other cause. He said nothing about it, though, feeling that it would be impolite to comment on it whether it was a reflection on the prosperity of the farm, or just on the frugality of its owner.

The conversation around the table was polite and relatively trivial until Mister Hillyard gave Arthur a significant glance and said, "Had some news from a passing post rider today that might be of interest to you."

Arthur stopped with his spoon halfway to his mouth, and set it back down, saying, "Oh? What is that?"

"Word from Pennsylvania is that the Congress has entered into a treaty of alliance with the French. It seems that the victory at Saratoga convinced King Louis that we have a fighting chance of winning this thing."

Arthur strained to keep his emotions off his face, willing himself to maintain a neutral expression. To speak so blithely of the death and destruction that had taken so much from him, as though it were just the strategic movement of a peg on a cribbage board, was unbelievable, and it was all he could do to not break into a rage.

Mister Hillyard continued, unaware of the younger man's internal struggle. "For now, it likely just means that they can be more open about supplying us with arms and powder, but perhaps it will amount to more in time. It's hoped that their navy will help us on the seas, and there's even word that they may be prevailed upon to send troops to aid our forces in the field."

He motioned diffidently with one hand at Arthur. "I understand that you're released from your service here once the war's over, so I thought that you might like to know that there is some light on the horizon in the direction of that peace."

Arthur mastered his urge to react outwardly, saying only, in as mild a tone as he could muster, "Peace is naturally to be hoped for, though you will pardon me for not cheering for the defeat of my own country."

Inwardly, though, he could feel shock and anger coursing through his veins. Those accursed French, taking advantage of the unrest in these colonies to put a knife in their long-time enemy's back! He had no doubt at all that what their pipsqueak king was actually after was vengeance for the French defeat in the late war. After all, they, like the English, had long memories and a long list of old grievances to settle.

And what would the French alliance mean in this effort to bring the rebellious colonies back under the proper dominion of the Crown? Would it, as Mister Hillyard presumed, bring the affair to a swift and unhappy conclusion? And if it did, how much of their supposed gains would the Americans be able to hold in the face of whatever French forces they welcomed with open arms? How long would it be until the French turned on them and took what they wanted from their erstwhile allies?

Mister Hillyard nodded thoughtfully. "I can understand how you would see it that way, my young friend, but perhaps it is better that the intercession of the French encourages your generals to depart an unwinnable fight without engagement than it is to suffer and inflict defeats on one another, until both your armies and our own are weakened to the point of collapse."

He shrugged. "I am no military tactician, but that is what I expect to happen."

Arthur nodded politely, but he knew that no British general would ever withdraw under the circumstances the American described, nor would the Crown direct them to do so. Honor, at least, would demand that they at least try the contest on the field.

What was that line from the play that the lieutenant was fond of quoting to him, about the happy few who fought on Saint Crispian's day? "Gentlemen in England now abed would think themselves accursed that they were not there?" Facing overwhelming odds and hoping to overcome them was simply a part of the heritage for which men like Arthur fought.

Mister Hillyard steepled his fingers as the silence grew. "Either way, I shall be a happy man. Should the war drag on, I have your service — and you have already proved to be wonderfully industrious — and if it comes to an early conclusion, why then, all of our privation and sacrifice will be at an end, and we will partake in the fruits of independence with trade unfettered by your Parliament's acts and taxes."

It almost felt to Arthur as though the man were needling him, trying to goad him into responding, but he maintained his polite expression, feigning interest in the farmer's ignorant and naïve opinions.

Arthur had no pretensions of being a statesman, but any fool could see that laws and taxes were an inevitable result of living under the protection of a sovereign. Whether that sovereign sat on the English throne or some farcical American one hardly mattered to someone at this remove from both, did it?

He chose to respond only to the compliment that the American had paid him. He smiled and said, "Thank you for your kind words, Mister Hillyard, and permit me to hope that

I will remain in your service for some time to come, under the circumstances."

The farmer looked startled for a moment, and then threw his head back and roared with laughter. "You nearly foxed me with that comment, son! I should invite you to dine with us more often, if you will be so entertaining at every dinner."

Arthur smiled tightly in reply, but said nothing more, picking up his spoon again and filling his mouth, lest something more caustic and less *entertaining* pass out of it.

The farmer's wife shot him a kind, understanding look, but before Arthur could make any sense of that, her husband turned to their daughter. "Your particular friend, Jack Contant, stopped by this morning. I've invited him for dinner after the Sunday service."

Miss Hillyard looked up sharply, her movement reminding Arthur of the sudden movement of a rabbit upon hearing a twig snap in the woods. "Mister Contant, you say?"

"Aye. He seemed to think that you and he got on famously on his last visit, and was hopeful of a longer visit this time. And, I need not remind you, his family owns the land adjoining this parcel in addition to their own farm, so there is the possibility of a fruitful combination at some time in the future."

Miss Hillyard appeared to be on the edge of saying something, and she glanced helplessly at her mother, who was studiously looking at her plate. Looking back down to her own plate, Miss Hillyard swallowed hard instead, her face looking a bit pale. "'Tis far too soon to be speaking of such matters, Papa."

Mister Hillyard only grunted in reply, so Missus Hillyard said, quietly, "There is no hurry, Gregory. Girls need to be given time for their feelings to blossom, without the harsh light of examination. Contant's parcel will be there tomorrow, just as it is today."

Arthur was suddenly very interested in his plate, after noticing that Miss Hillyard was no longer pale, but appeared to have flushed bright red. Or perhaps it was just the light from the sunset. Either way, it was high time for him to finish eating and retreat to the barn.

On his pallet that night, Arthur reflected on the dinner, wondering at both items that Mister Hillyard had related at the table. He heard a scratching at the door to his stall, and stood up to let in the grey tabby who had made a habit out of visiting him.

He laid back down and stroked the cat's ears when it curled up on his chest. His mind was not on the animal, though, but had returned to the news of the day.

He'd heard that the Americans were getting all manner of irregular help from many of England's longtime enemies. It seemed as though this little rebellion was an excuse for every out-of-work noble with pretensions of military prowess to come and prove himself. A few, he'd heard grudgingly admitted over campfires, had turned out to be equal to their billing.

The Frenchman Lafayette, of course, had surprised everyone by becoming an effective aide-de-camp to the American's General Washington. Arthur had heard, too, that it was a Polish officer — he couldn't remember or pronounce the man's name for anything — who had been instrumental in frustrating the pursuit of the Americans after Ticonderoga.

He wished that he could remember the man's name, if only to more effectively curse him. Arthur's squad had set out in formation with the rest of the army down a road that was already rough from neglect. They'd started to set a good pace, only to find that the enemy had felled tree after tree across their path, which raised everyone's ire.

What had likely taken but a few minutes to drop upon the road cost Arthur and his squad absurd amounts of effort and time to clear, every time it was their turn to remove the obstacles.

When the army came to the first burned-out bridge, a collective groan arose from all who saw it, and not a few choice words were shouted before the officers could restore order. It wasn't until later that Arthur learned — and promptly forgot — the name of the man who'd come to America from Europe to help frustrate the Crown in its attempt to hold the colonies.

Eventually, the generals gave up battling the Americans' tactic of using axes and flames to fight the British army to a standstill from a safe remove, and orders came down directing the construction of a new road. Arthur could hardly see what that gained them, other than some degree of surprise, but at least they were able to move forward at a predictably steady — if reduced — pace.

Spain and Holland had each been helping the Americans in their own way with supplies and secretive advice, so with the French now openly declared for America, how long would it take England's other enemies to add their own voices to the din? It seemed that the King and Parliament had managed to make enemies of the entire world, and Arthur felt the first hint of doubt that the Crown was on the right side of the question of American independence.

He set that thought firmly aside, though, and turned to

pondering Miss Hillyard's strange reaction to the presumed suitor Mister Hillyard had brought up. In a countryside with so few young men in it that farmers had to hire enemy soldiers for labor, having an eligible youth as a neighbor seemed fortuitous indeed.

Yet, Miss Hillyard seemed startled that her father had invited Mister Contant to dine at their table, and evinced no particular enthusiasm at the prospect of his bid for her hand.

It was more than mere reluctance, too. There had been an hint of fear in her eyes when his name was mentioned, and though it was none of his affair, Arthur could not help but ruminate on what might have been behind that until sleep claimed him for the night, the cat purring happily atop him and sharing his warmth.

Chapter 4

Picking stone was tedious and backbreaking. Picking out weeds and pests, though, was positively stifling. Add the rising summer heat and the fact that Mister Hillyard insisted on mixing several different crops in the same field, and Arthur's frustration by noontime was nearly a thing that he could pick up and throw by itself.

Miss Hillyard had established the pleasant habit of bringing him switchel around midday every day, which gave him an excuse to pause and find some shade for a few minutes.

She brought a cup for herself some days, and they talked quietly about the news of the war, or shared gossip about her neighbors, or she answered his questions about how to perform work for which her father had only given him the barest sketch of instructions.

She appeared comfortable in his company, and seemed to enjoy hearing his stories of the doomed campaign that had found its ignoble end at Saratoga. He was careful not to overly vilify the Americans who'd opposed them, as he was coming to suspect that she was, in her quiet way, a fierce partisan for the American rebellion.

Arthur supposed that the desire for independence must have simply seeped into these people from the water of New-England, so universally it appeared in his conversations with them.

This particular day, Miss Hillyard handed him his cup and said with a cautious note to her tone, "There is news today that I feel you will not welcome, but which I think you ought know."

He swallowed a gulp and gave her a long-suffering look. "Have the King's men yielded utterly to your armies' advances, and the end of the war looms close?"

She gave him an exasperated huff. "Not exactly, but there is word that your General Clinton has withdrawn from our capital city of Philadelphia, and is on the march northward."

Arthur looked up sharply. "He's abandoned Philadelphia? For what cause? Have you armies in the field still near there that have sent him flying?"

Miss Hillyard shrugged. "I know not, only that Philadelphia has been freed, and Papa seems to think that it is a step toward the eventual success of the entire war."

Arthur frowned, looking away toward the barn as he thought. He said, suddenly, "General Clinton left our forces at Saratoga to twist in the wind, when he was supposed to have come to our relief. Twice, in fact — first before we capitulated, and then a second time afterward, when General Burgoyne had relied on Clinton's proximity to weigh on the negotiations for the terms of the convention. It is his doing in part that I came to be in your father's service."

She sipped slowly at her cup, lost in thought herself for a long moment. Finally, she said, quietly, "Then it should be quite fitting, in an ironical way, should his actions be a step toward your departure from Papa's service, would it not?" Arthur thought that her tone belied some sadness at the prospect, though he doubted that it was for any reason other than that the family would miss his labor about the farm."

He pursed his lips. "I should not be so optimistic about the withdrawal from Philadelphia portending any early exit from these colonies. Everybody knew that the primary reason for striving for that city was to capture your Congress. Once they were found to have taken to the countryside, I would suppose that it no longer made a strategic stronghold."

He scowled, adding, "'Tis passing strange that they marched out, though, instead of simply embarking from there for their next place of duty. Are the French already in control of the seas, I wonder?"

"I know nothing of this, either, but it may be that your armies have some other objective in mind, as well. Who can know what generals are playing at, save other generals?"

Arthur smiled grimly and drained the rest of his cup. "Not even they are granted any special understanding of one another, from what I saw in the campaign I was engaged in. Certainly General Clinton and General Burgoyne failed to come to any meeting of the minds."

She smiled back and accepted the empty cup from him. "Well, they are but men, and most men are but passing competent at understanding one another under the best of circumstances."

He nodded thoughtfully. "True enough. The circumstances under which our generals operate are hardly the best possible, either, what with having to bring armies from across the ocean, and being obliged to supply them from an unwelcoming countryside. Add to that your 'minute-men' taking shots at them from behind every fencerow and your armies harrying them and their messengers."

He shrugged. "It's a wonder that they should ever manage

a coordinated thought within their own heads, never mind coordinated action across a battlefield." He smiled in an attempt to soften his words, but a gathering storm was evident on her face regardless.

"Our men would have no interest in your generals or their messengers, were they not here to impose the Parliament's fell will upon us on your vaunted battlefields. If your generals — to say nothing of your Parliament — should put greater effort into understanding the legitimate complaints of these colonies than to reducing us to utter subjugation, we might all profit from the outcome." Her tone was frosty, but he could hardly leave her accusations unanswered.

He replied, as mildly as he could, "If your Congress had put a little effort into understanding why they owe their allegiance to their King, instead of to some abstract notions of the 'pursuit of happiness,' we could have avoided all of this unpleasantness entirely."

Miss Hillyard's voice rose to a near shout. "Unpleasantness, you call it? Reducing whole towns to ashes by naval bombardment, offering no quarter to defeated men, dumping our captured soldiers onto prison ships to pray for the release of death is far more than *unpleasantness*, Mister Leary. It is outright barbarism, and I am quite shocked to hear your dismiss it so lightly."

Her expression was furious now, and before he had a chance to explain that he'd meant no harm in his comments, she whirled away and was marching back into the house, her back held straight and her head high.

Arthur stood for a moment, looking at the door that she had slammed behind herself, and then shook his head and sighed, walking back into the field to continue at his labors.

The litany of horrors that Miss Hillyard had recited sounded like the rumormongering of a ruthless propagandist trying to whip up sentiment against an enemy.

Certainly, the Crown's forces had exerted necessary violence where it was called for, but they behaved themselves as befit facing traitors to the King. Indeed, being held prisoner pending parole was better than the gallows that might otherwise be promised in payment for treason.

As for the reduction of enemy coastal emplacements, Arthur guessed that any naval bombardment would look like savagery to the innocent eye of a civilian — and would make for lurid broadsheets and feigned outrage from the erstwhile leaders of the rebellion.

That evening, it was Missus Hillyard, not her daughter, who brought his supper out to his quarters. "Constance is not feeling herself this afternoon, Mister Leary, and she asked me to bring you your meal."

He replied, automatically, "I do hope that she is feeling better tomorrow."

Missus Hillyard grimaced. "I misdoubt that she will, as Mister Hillyard has invited that Contant boy over for supper again, and never mind that our Constance only sat with him because she knows how much her Papa desires a combination between our families — and our land holdings."

She shook herself, seeming to remember suddenly that Arthur was merely a hired hand, and not a confidant. "Oh, pay me no mind, gossiping with you about our family matters. You can set your dishes outside the kitchen door when you're finished eating, and Constance or I will pick them up when we rise to get breakfast tomorrow."

"Thank you, Missus Hillyard," Arthur said. "Please let Miss Hillyard know that I hope that whatever is troubling her is but a passing malady."

"Oh, I will, Mister Leary. You are so kind to say so. 'Tis a pity . . ."

She trailed off, but Arthur suddenly felt certain that he knew what was left unsaid. It was a pity that he was British, a pity that he was a soldier, a pity that his station in life — which had seemed so fine to him when he'd first put on a proper uniform, but was now little better than any indenture — was not equal to Constance's, who would someday bring her husband a fine and valuable farm.

And so, it was a pity that Missus Leary could not engage in any sort of machinations to persuade him — or her daughter, or her husband — that he was a fit replacement for the neighbor's son as a potential match.

He nodded, acknowledging the unspoken thought. "Good night, Missus Hillyard, and thank you for bringing my supper out."

As he ate mechanically, barely even tasting the food on his plate, he thought about the conversation with Miss Hillyard that afternoon, and wished that he had been able to anticipate just how vehement her attachment to the cause of American independence would be.

Although he was not about to change his mind — these colonies had cost the Crown centuries of blood and treasure, and so owed the King perhaps a greater degree of allegiance than did most of his subjects — angering his hosts was impolite, at the least. At the worst, it could threaten the relative comfort and safety he'd found here in their service.

The prospect returning to the barracks at Cambridge caused a cold chill to run down his back, and he shuddered in spite of the still-warm evening air. He resolved to let no further word of criticism of the American cause pass his lips, no matter how comfortable and easy it seemed to tease back and forth with Mister Hillyard's daughter over the matter.

After he was finished eating, Arthur lay down with the grey cat on his chest, and set himself the disagreeable task of trying to see the behavior of the British forces through her eyes.

It was true that he had heard it suggested that surrendering American forces need not be offered the honors of war, nor deserved the standing of a legitimate enemy soldier. The rationalization given was that they had each, individually and as a company, engaged in treason and insurrection.

These were not the acts of a belligerent recognized nation, but common crimes, proscribed under the law, and so when these rebels were brought to justice, they deserved no regard under the common practices of war.

Remembering the moment as though he stood again in the sun watching General Burgoyne accept the return of his sword from the American general, Arthur realized that the enemy forces were behaving in a manner that was appropriate to the conduct of the army of a civilized nation . . . that they were behaving better than the British, in that regard.

The thought left him breathless for a moment, and shook his certainty in the moral superiority of the British cause. He set that aside quickly, not eager to consider it fully. He still retained the conviction that these subjects of the King owed at least the same allegiance to the Crown as did his own neighbors back home.

He shook his head to dispel the disquieting arguments playing themselves out there, and returned to pondering the news that Miss Hillyard had shared with him before the conversation went all wrong.

He'd worried over it all afternoon. Despite the quip he'd made to Constance, he was not aware of Clinton being so shy of facing action that he would fly with his army at the merest word of an approaching American force.

Of course, the very idea that a British army had anything to fear from a colonial rabble under arms would have been unthinkable, before General Burgoyne's defeat at Saratoga. Perhaps the shock of that, and the desire to avoid sharing in Burgoyne's shame, had led the other general to abandon Philadelphia.

And, perhaps, Arthur's defensive remark about Philadelphia not being worth the trouble to hold it once the Congress had slipped through the fingers of the British had been more true than not. It was, after all, widely known to be one of the centers of the American rebellion, and doubtless the sentiment of the residents ran strongly against their occupiers.

He was not well studied on how the city was situated for defensive purposes, nor even whether it controlled any important accesses to the rest of the colonies, but it could well be that its only real military significance had been the presence of the capital there. If that were the case, then once the capital was elsewhere, there was no further justification for tying down a whole army just to hold a city.

The fact that Clinton's army had marched away overland was somewhat troubling at first blush, but as nothing was yet known of their destination, a land march may simply have been the most efficient route available. It was also possible, as Arthur had mused to Miss Hillyard, that the French had already asserted such control of the seas as to preclude moving the army in transports, but Arthur knew that given his druthers, he would opt for the march every time.

He fell asleep still thinking of the implications of the news, and of Miss Hillyard's fury at him. His dreams were unsettled, as had often been the case after the horror of the battlefield outside Saratoga, but he was able to dispel them well enough to get some sleep before the cock crowed.

Chapter 5

"We will start today with sweeping out the barn," Mister Hillyard said, though Arthur was only able to give him part of his attention. His mind was buzzing with the task of making sense of Constance's breakfast delivery.

He'd slept through sunrise, which was unusual enough, so he was still abed when she knocked at the stall door to bring in his food. She didn't wait for his response, but entered almost immediately, setting his food down with perhaps more of a pronounced thump on the table than was strictly necessary.

He sat up, dislodging the cat and blinking sleep out of his eyes, and when he could see clearly enough, he found her standing with her fists balled on her hips, and a glare on her face.

"You will not speak ill to me again of our cause. I know some who have served nobly as minute-men, ensuring that farms like ours need not fear that they will be overrun, either by your King's men, or by any Indians who they may incite to violence against us. I have also known men who have marched away with the militia, never to return."

She wiped angrily at her face before continuing, and Arthur was amazed to realize that she was crying. "We are on different sides of this war, you and I, and I had permitted myself to forget that, hoping that you were coming to see the need for our independency in the course of living among us. I see now that I was wrong, and that in your heart, you still regard us as subjects to be reduced to our prior state of servitude. Well, we will not tolerate that outcome, and the sooner you understand that, the happier your remaining time on these shores will be."

Gathering his wits as well as he could with his mind still fogged from sleep, Arthur said, hesitantly, "I truly meant no offense, and I have already resolved to choose my words more carefully." When she nodded briskly in answer, crossing her arms over herself still in evident pique, he continued, "It is true that it is my duty to hope for the return of these colonies to *their* duty to the King I serve, but I am not here with the aim of imposing servitude on anyone."

He did not dare give voice to the fact that he had begun to admit to himself some doubts about the means through which the quest to reunite the restive colonies with their sovereign was being pursued, but opted to attempt to mollify Miss Hillyard by a different line of argument.

He smiled gently and motioned around himself. "As you may have noted, it is I who am now in a condition of servitude, and I will confess that I am grateful for it. Working on your father's farm is better than being a captive in the barracks, hoping to avoid the onset of camp fever. And, despite all that I represent, I appreciate your kindness to me, and I beg your pardon for the offense that I caused you."

Arthur was gratified to note that Miss Hillyard seemed to relax her stance ever so slightly before she said, "For my part, I ask that you understand that my anger is not directed at you so much as it is at the acts of the Parliament that I have heard my

Papa discuss so often with guests at our table. You are merely the convenient target of that anger."

She motioned to his food with a jerk of her head. "Your breakfast is getting cold."

As she turned to leave, he called after her, "Can we yet be friends?"

She had stopped and looked over her shoulder at him for a moment, coolly contemplating him. "I suppose I can concede that much."

"Are you hearing a thing I'm saying to you, Mister Leary?" Arthur was jerked back into the moment by Mister Hillyard's sharp tone.

"Oh, aye, Mister Hillyard. I'm to ensure that the pasture gates are all secured before I turn the cows out, and the goats are to be led individually to their paddock, lest they escape."

"Mind that you tie up the goat's pen with a proper knot, too, just as though you were from the navy rather than the army." Mister Hillyard flashed a quick smile, seeming to try to soften his words.

Arthur favored the farmer with a lopsided grin. "Though the men of the sail may know a greater variety of knots, and the advantages of each, I've had no small experience with securing tents and the like with rope myself. I can tie a proper knot."

"Very well, then. My daughter will be busy all day cooking supper for a guest, so I'll expect you to perform this chore with all of the care that she would have given it, were she not otherwise engaged."

"I understand, Mister Hillyard." He managed to keep the grimace that wanted to crease his face under control, as he recalled that Missus Hillyard had told him the guest was to be the neighbor's son, whom Miss Hillyard did not care for.

He felt a wave of compassion for her, then, realizing that part of her outburst at him yesterday had likely been due to her anxiety over her father's plans for her.

It was not his place to question his host's management of his own family, but it seemed to Arthur that Mister Hillyard was too much consumed with the thought of the advantages to himself of combining his holdings with his neighbor's, and not enough with the question of whether his daughter's heart was open to being joined to that of his neighbor's son.

These somber thoughts occupied his mind as he busied himself with the tasks that Mister Hillyard had set him to. The job of moving the animals to where they were to be penned while he worked went smoothly enough, although the goats were — as was their wont — rambunctious as he led them to their enclosure.

Cleaning the barn was not hard work, just tedious. He did manage to step into a pile of goat droppings in a poorly-lit corner, but otherwise, even dealing with the animal waste wasn't as much hard work as was weeding, and the morning fairly flew by.

When Miss Hillyard brought him his midday switchel, she did not bring out a cup for herself, and did not tarry to talk, but neither was she cold with him — only hurried, as she instructed him, "Bring the cup back to the door when you are finished with it. I must tend to my cooking for company tonight."

She did not look either particularly happy nor unhappy about the prospect of hosting Mister Contant, just concerned about setting him a respectable table.

Arthur found himself wishing that her conduct reflected

more of the reservations about the neighbor's son that her mother seemed to think she had, and without quite knowing why, he was in a foul mood the rest of the afternoon.

His mood was not improved in the slightest when one of the goats slipped away from him as he was trying to return it to the clean barn, and immediately went running for the hills just as Mister Hillyard came out of the house to witness the creature's flight. The farmer's face went stern and he pointed after the goat, shouting, "Well, go and catch him! What are you waiting for?"

Arthur had hesitated because under the terms of his leave to come and work here, he was not to depart the bounds of Mister Hillyard's property, on pain of being returned to the barracks, and even imprisonment in the gaol, depending upon the circumstances.

However, he knew also that to fail to follow the instructions of the farmer would have consequences of all sorts, so he sprinted off after the beast.

The wily creature either saw or heard him behind itself, and seemed to find new reserves of speed as it dashed toward the wooded ridge behind the farm. It leapt over a stone wall with hardly any hesitation, while Arthur had to slow down and clamber over the piled stones.

By the time Arthur caught sight of it again, the animal was stuck firmly in a bramble, bleating piteously.

Although the dense raspberry bushes held the goat immobile so that Arthur could catch up with it, getting in to where it stood trembling cost him any number of painful encounters with the thorny vines.

Finally, he made his way in far enough to be able to reach the lead that the animal had yanked out of his hand in his bid for freedom.

He wrapped the rope securely around his wrist and waded further through the brambles so that he could reach in and untangle the vines wrapped around the goat's body, some of which were tight enough for the thorns to have drawn blood.

By the time he emerged, half-carrying the goat until he reached open ground again, Mister Hillyard had caught up and was favoring both man the animal with pursed lips.

He shook his head with an air of disappointment. "It's not the first time that George has gotten the better of one of us, but he is worse off than usual for his little adventure."

Arthur set the animal down on the ground and looked him over. He could see trickles of blood staining the goat's fur in several places. He might have felt more compassion if he weren't aware of at least as many places where his own skin was torn and bleeding.

Mister Hillyard sighed, taking in Arthur's condition at a glance. "Well, bring him back, and then get yourself washed up. Take some time to ensure that you get all of the thorns out of your skin. Raspberries as overgrown as these are worth avoiding, for those thorns will fester. I'll have Missus Hillyard bring you an ointment that may help."

He looked down at the goat. "As for George, there's not much we can do, and maybe this will teach him not to go off on adventures." Arthur glared down at the beast, which looked barely chastened by its minor injuries.

After he'd washed and returned to his room, Arthur opened the stall door for Missus Hillyard, who tutted and fussed over his scratched and perforated arms and hands.

He waved her away, taking the bowl of ointment from her.

"Thank you very kindly, but I'll apply this myself. Some of my wounds are in places where that should be tended to in privacy."

Missus Hillyard colored slightly and smiled nervously as she left. "I'll tell Constance to be sure to knock before she brings you your supper."

Arthur felt a flush steal over his own face and he nodded wordlessly, closing the door. Whatever was in the ointment stung even worse than the brambles themselves, and it was only the knowledge that Miss Hillyard might at any moment be within earshot that restrained his tongue from uttering the most vile oaths he'd learned from his fellow soldiers during his time in uniform.

Chapter 6

Despite being served on his solitary table in the coarse confines of his stall in the barn, dinner that night was remarkable, a delicately-raised pie, rich in meat and hoarded vegetables, and topped with a caudle that smelled of good sack wine and spices. Alongside the pie was a firm pudding, spooned over with more of the caudle, and his tin cup was full of good cider for a change from the usual evening share of switchel.

Miss Hillyard was wearing her nicest skirts and an intricately-embroidered bodice that Arthur hadn't seen before. "You look very fine tonight," he felt bold enough to say as she turned to leave after putting his meal on the table.

She smiled distractedly and answered, "Papa insisted that I dress for our guest tonight. I think I look as though I am pretending at being one of the fine ladies of Boston society, but Papa seems satisfied, and it costs me only a little effort beyond the usual to accommodate his wishes."

"I have not seen the ladies in Boston, but I have no doubt that you would put them to shame, were you to appear among their number this evening."

She dipped her head in acknowledgment of the compliment. "I thank you very kindly, and would hear more of your pretty words, but I have to get the table prepared before our guest arrives. Good evening, Mister Leary."

She'd hurried back to the house then, holding her skirts up to keep them out of the dust.

Arthur sat down and tucked into his meal, savoring every bite. If he had been able to whisper into the ear of a footsore Corporal Leary as he shuffled through the snow from Saratoga to Cambridge with his stomach knotted in hunger, and inform him that a meal such as this lay in his future, he knew that the unbelieving laughter would be echoing still.

When he finished eating and had tossed back the last drops of the cider, he gathered up his dishes, unsure whether he was expected to leave them at the door to his quarters, or bring them to the house as had become his habit. He decided to set them outside his quarters, so as to avoid disturbing the family as they welcomed a guest.

Stepping outside, Arthur saw a young man striding down the road, and he paused to examine the youth, whom he assumed was the neighbor's son, Jack Contant.

For the son of a mere country farmer, he walked with a swagger that made Arthur's eyes roll involuntarily. Like some of the dandies who had come to bid on labor contracts all those weeks before, his elaborately-trimmed cocked hat was decorated with a showy white plume. The feather bobbed as the man strode along, and Arthur could not help but feel sorry for the bird that had sacrificed its plumage for such an obvious popinjay.

From this distance, Arthur could not clearly make out the other man's features, but he had a general impression of a florid complexion, unbound dark hair lying heavily upon his collar, and a cocksure tilt of his head as he looked up at the house he was approaching.

Contant — for that was obviously who it was — walked to the door, and almost immediately Mister Hillyard threw it open, his daughter at his side. Arthur thought Miss Hillyard caught sight of him standing by the barn, for it looked as though she gave a tiny shake of her head in his direction before she closed the door.

His mind filled with unease, Arthur hurriedly set down his dishes and returned to his quarters, where he tried to go to sleep as the dusk gathered. Between the bramble scratches and the itching from the drying ointment on his skin, he struggled mightily to find a comfortable position, tossing and turning on his pallet. The grey cat gave up on him entirely after he disturbed her for the fourth time, and left with a disapproving twitch of her tail at the door.

After it had gotten full dark, it seemed he had just dropped off into sleep when he awoke from a terrible dream to what sounded like a gunshot, which brought him upright on his pallet with a jerk.

His nightmare had been on a familiar theme, of being dragged by some unseen being away from his unit where their encampment stood outside of Saratoga, This time, though, in addition to his own screams as his fingers dug furrows in the earth, he had looked over to see Miss Hillyard being dragged away beside him, and her screams were louder even than his own, so loud that they almost seemed real.

The report that had woken Arthur from his dream had immediately stopped whatever inexorable force was dragging him along the ground, and in his confusion on waking so suddenly, he felt as though he'd been dropped from the rafters of the barn back down onto his pallet.

Outside, he could hear Mister Hillyard shouting into the

darkness, though he could not make out what the farmer was saying. He hurriedly pulled on his trousers to see what was the matter, and to ask whether his host needed some help from him.

When Arthur emerged from the barn, the moon was midway up in the sky, and low clouds scudded across its face, permitting him to just see where Mister Hillyard stood at the road where it passed closest to the house, his nightshirt loose over his knees, and his musket visible in his hand as a long, dark shadow.

He was staring off into the darkness down the road when Arthur emerged from the barn, but he turned at the sound of the door, which swung shut behind Arthur, banging on the frame. He shouted hoarsely, "Get back into your room, Mister Leary and don't you stir until morning. This doesn't concern you, and you can only come to grief if you attempt to involve yourself. Get back into the barn, and bar the door."

Arthur was shocked at the man's words and even more, how he sounded. He wondered whether there had been some sort of attempt made to raid the farm for forage . . . and if so, whether it had been a British or American force.

He knew well enough that when supplies ran low, the countryside around an army could come to be regarded as an adjunct to the commissary, and that it didn't matter much if the landholders were friend or foe.

As he reluctantly followed Mister Hillyard's instructions, though, he realized that he ought to have heard any such intruders first, as they would likely have gone directly to the barn, bypassing the house entirely. This was where there was livestock to pilfer, and barns often held supplies of grain and other stores, besides. They also had the advantage of usually being unoccupied, so a party of soldiers intent on securing supplies could do their work unimpeded.

Not that such a raid was without risk, of course, as he had observed first-hand in the course of the army's campaign. At one point on the road to Saratoga, Arthur had been grumbling with one of his men about short rations, when the sergeant ambled over and inserted himself into their conversation.

"Don't you worry none about supplies," he said to Arthur, including the other soldier with a meaningful look. "General Burgoyne's got a plan."

He looked around as though checking for eavesdroppers, and then said, "He's sending one of those German regiments out to go and take what we need from the rebels. It's not a secret, exactly, but we don't want to post notices on every tree, either." He grinned, and Arthur couldn't help smiling in reply, anticipating the coming improvement in their rations.

A week later, the remnants of the German regiment came straggling back without their general, and stories of the defeat they had suffered at the hands of the New-England forces ran like wildfire through the encampment. Even Arthur's normally taciturn sergeant seemed shocked.

"It's one matter to have to retreat from an ungentlemanly attack, and the dear Lord knows that these devils have no respect for the accepted norms of battlefield conduct. But to have so many men lost from a mere supply-gathering assignment . . ." He shook his head, poking at the squad's fire beside which he'd crouched to speak with them. "It's unnerving, it is, and I don't mind telling you that. These colonials have been said to be no good in the field, but the jägers we lost were almost as good as any British unit."

Needless to say, the rations had not gotten appreciably better — and worse, everyone's morale seemed to have been shaken. Between the frustration of having their way blocked by clever destruction, and now this, it was little wonder that by the time they did reach Saratoga, they were primed for defeat there.

This evening's upset didn't have the feeling of a foraging raid gone bad, though, so after he closed and secured the door, he attempted to satisfy his curiosity, peeking out through a gap between the door and its frame. Arthur could see Mister Hillyard survey the fields around the farm one last time, and then trudge back to the house, looking somehow small and defeated, his shoulders low and his chin against his chest, the gun cradled uselessly in his arms. Arthur could make no sense of the man's actions or demeanor, and though he returned to his pallet as instructed, he only dozed fitfully all the rest of the night.

In the morning, he awoke to the cock's crow as usual, but there was none of the ordinary cheerful morning bustle evident within the house. Arthur was accustomed to waking fully with the delivery of his breakfast by a smiling Constance or a harried Missus Hillyard, but neither of them appeared, although the grey cat paid him a brief visit before her ears perked up at some small creature scurrying in the rafters, and she left quickly in pursuit.

Stretching and pulling on his clothes, he went outside to investigate the state of his hosts. A small curl of smoke, fitfully pulled into oblivion from the top of the chimney by a passing breeze, was the only sign that anyone even resided in the house, and he wasn't sure whether it was his duty to return to his quarters until otherwise instructed, or to see what was the matter. He opted to return to his stall, and sat on the stool, cleaning dried-on mud from the welts in his boot soles. He made a mental note to sweep out the debris before it earned him a disappointed frown from Constance.

When the sun had fully risen and there was still no sign of the family, Arthur dared to approach the kitchen door and knock. After a long pause, he heard a shuffle of movement within, and Missus Hillyard opened it, appearing mussed and puffy-eyed.

She looked at Arthur for a moment and then mumbled, "There'll be no breakfast today, I'll warrant. We've none of us slept a wink all night, and Mister Hillyard is caring for Constance."

Arthur's heart hammered within his chest as he stammered, "Wh-what has happened to her?"

Missus Hillyard seemed to debate answering for a long time. Finally, she took a deep breath and looked him in the eye. "I may as well tell you, as I suppose you'll learn sooner or later. She is not badly injured, aside from some bruises and scratches, but while they were keeping company with each other after Mister Hillyard and I had retired for the evening, Mister Contant forced himself on her."

Chapter 7

The moment a rebel's bullet had passed close enough by his ear to buzz like an angry hornet, during the final battle at Saratoga, was the only other time in his life when Arthur could remember everything being so still, as though the world had stopped while his mind leapt ahead and absorbed what was happening.

He was aware of the lazy beating of his heart in the seconds both moments, and both times he felt it leap into a frenzy within his chest. The normally reassuring solidity of the ground under his feet seemed as illusory as that upon the deck of a waddling troop transport on the Atlantic Ocean.

His own sharp gasp sounded harsh and distant to his ears, and he could barely hear it over the roaring in his head.

"He . . . he hurt her?"

Missus Hillyard gave him a pitying look. "Oh, aye. Worse than that, he insulted her honor, which will be a harder thing to knit back together."

Arthur placed one hand at the top of the door frame and leaned on it while he took a few breaths and gathered himself.

It was not his place to feel this way about an insult to his employer's daughter. She was no more than a friend to him — if even barely that much. He told himself that he must be reacting this way because he could not bear to see any woman so abused.

The violation of her parents' trust, as well as hers, was unforgivable . . . but it was not his to forgive.

Why, then, did the thought make him want to run down the road in the direction Mister Hillyard had been glaring into the night, until he found someone who might answer for this crime? Why did he hope that he might find a crumpled body where the farmer's bullet had felled the villain, that he might abuse the corpse further with boots and stones?

He entertained the briefest vision of Contant's hat trampled into a flat, unrecognizable mass, and Contant's face treated likewise under it. He almost launched himself out the door to make the vision a reality — how many neighbors' houses might he have to visit before he found the cocky young man and his hat? — before he mastered himself and forced his fists to release their involuntary clench.

There were better ways for him to be of service to his hosts, ways that did not raise the question of him mistaking his place in their lives. He was a servant, not a member of the family.

He controlled his wild thoughts, he realized that here was an opportunity — and an obligation — to serve them.

He shook his head heavily and stood up straight. "Will you permit me to make breakfast for us all, so that you may all regain your strength and health? I know that Mister Hillyard bid my contract for my back, and not for any ability at the hearth, but I should like very much to be of service as I may in your time of need."

Missus Hillyard considered him for a moment, and then stood aside, making space for him to enter the house. "I will return to my daughter's side. I trust that you can find your way around the kitchen without my guidance."

Arthur nodded, though in truth, under any other circumstances, he would want advice and guidance before working at someone else's hearth. As it was, he applied himself to the tasks at hand with grim determination to not unnecessarily disturb Missus Hillyard.

He closed the door behind himself and surveyed the kitchen briefly as she disappeared into the front room. He added kindling from the basket beside the firebox to the coals, still banked from the prior evening, and carefully built it up to a decent cooking fire. Investigating the casks that stood along one wall, he found one that contained meal, and started on making a porridge. Arthur wasn't sure of the proportions, but he set a kettle to boil on the crane, swinging it over the flames after filling it to the halfway point with water.

He remembered a time in the Cambridge barracks when all they could get was some meal, and the man who had been in charge of cooking had added a bit of molasses to it, rendering the porridge both more nutritious and more satisfying to the palate.

Arthur checked the other casks thoroughly, but could find none that contained the ingredient, so he shrugged and told himself that good enough would have to do in this circumstance.

Once the kettle was bubbling, he swung it back out where he could reach it without singeing himself and stirred in several handfuls of meal with a wooden spoon he'd found hanging on a peg beside the chimney, until the porridge started to feel as though it would thicken. He returned it to sit partially over the heat, stirring it vigorously so it would not stick.

Throughout the process, he tried to let the challenges of

working in an unfamiliar kitchen with unknown ingredients and tools consume his mind, but his thoughts kept returning to Constance. He forcefully redirected his mind from the events she had suffered the night before, which left him pondering how angry she had been at him earlier in the day over what now seemed like a trivial disagreement.

How could he have provoked her so, when she had shown him nothing but kindness and consideration? Though she'd said that she would put aside her anger with him, had that in some way contributed to her finding herself in a compromising position with her assailant?

If he'd been more accommodating of his current position in this society, even to the point of keeping quiet about his loyalty to the Crown, might this Mister Contant's suit for her have been easier for her to rebuff? Could Arthur's presence as an obedient and tractable servant have given Constance an argument to convince her father that there were other options than the neighbor's dandy son?

He shook his head to dispel the unproductive direction in which those thoughts led, and gave the porridge one last vicious stir before swinging it off the flames. At least that had done as he intended, and was nearly thick enough form him to stand the spoon in it and have it stay upright.

Casting about the kitchen, he finally located where the tinware was kept, and spooned porridge into the first of four bowls, hissing and cursing to himself as the thin metal immediately passed the heat of the boiling-hot food to his fingers.

He set the bowl down on the table and waved his fingers in the air in an attempt to cool them. When the pain in his fingertips had subsided a bit, he used the tail of his shirt to insulate his fingers as he filled the other three bowls, setting each of them on the table in turn.

Finding where the dining spoons were kept required him to root through drawers and baskets all about the kitchen, which made him feel like a cutpurse digging through a stranger's belongings in search of coins. Finally, though, he discovered the utensils hanging in plain sight on the wall over the casks, and he took down four of those.

He'd spotted a large serving-tray while looking around the kitchen, and he transferred three of the bowls to that, and carried it into the house proper, unsure where he'd need to go next.

The front room was dim and quiet, shutters still closed against the low morning sun. He could see only a couple of empty chairs and a small settee, which was lying on its back, exposing its six stout legs like some grotesque bug overset on the floor.

His blood ran cold in his face as he realized that this must be the very scene of the violation against Constance, and he turned away, finding the stairs to the top floor behind him. He steeled his nerves and ventured up them, tucking his elbows in to avoid spilling the tray.

In the small hallway at the top of the stairs, light spilled from an open door. He stopped before it and called out softly, "I've a makeshift porridge here for you all."

Missus Hillyard answered, "Bring it in, Mister Leary, if you would be so kind."

As he entered the bedroom, the first thing he noticed was Constance's form huddled at the far side of her bed, leaning against the hunched-over figure of her father, who sat beside her. Neither of them stirred to look at him, but Missus Hillyard's eyes found his, and she motioned with her head at the small writing desk under the window.

Arthur proceeded carefully in that direction, keeping his eyes directed to his steps and his destination. He set the tray down on the desktop with a minimum of clattering, and turned to face Missus Hillyard.

She was again focused solely on her daughter and husband, seeming barely aware that he was even in the room.

He stole a glance at Constance, whose face he could see from where he stood. Her eyes were swollen and red from tears shed over the course of hours, and an angry red welt the size and shape of a man's hand marked her cheek. She did not seem to see him, and Arthur tore his gaze away as quickly as he could, but he knew that he would never be able to get the image out of his mind.

He bowed to excuse himself, even though nobody in it was even aware that he was there at all, and hurried out, maintaining his composure until he was down the stairs and back into the kitchen.

As hot tears streaked his cheeks, he remonstrated himself for reacting so sharply to seeing Constance hurt.

After all, he had seen men shot through on the battlefield — had watched men die before his eyes — and had not felt so affected as he did now. He had dug graves for close companions, and had shed fewer tears than now overflowed his eyes.

However, a soldier laying down his life for his cause was fulfilling the duty he'd said he was willing to undertake. Falling ill of camp fevers, being shot by an enemy, even drowning or freezing while en route . . . those were all risks that one accepted when taking the recruiter's bounty and signing on the line.

Constance had not offered to bear this risk when she had prepared supper and welcomed a guest into her home. She should not have had to pay the price for her father's wish for a business combination with the adjoining parcel of land.

Indeed, was it not part of the job of a soldier to protect innocent girls from this sort of disorder and violence? Was that not what had sent him here to these colonies, to maintain the Crown's rule of law and its authority to prosecute wrongdoers over even the most resistant of its subjects?

Of course, the force he was a part of had failed in its mission, and even were he still in the uniform of His Majesty's army, the administration of justice would be a task that fell to other men. It had been his job to ensure the conditions that might have prevented such lawlessness. Still, he felt a sharp moment of anger at the rebellion that had removed Crown authority from this community, exposing a girl like Constance to the uncouth appetites of a neighbor's son.

He wiped his eyes impatiently on the sleeve of his shirt, and shook his head violently to dispel such thoughts from his head. Then he picked up his bowl and spoon from the kitchen table and brought them to his quarters, where he ate and he tried to force himself to forget the dull, unseeing glaze in Constance's eyes, and the events that had put it there.

After he broke his fast, he dressed and attended to those chores he knew innately must be done daily around the farm. The animals needed feeding, eggs needed gathering, pests needed to be removed from the plants in the fields, and water needed to be fetched up from the pond for all. The disruptions of human events could not be allowed to interrupt the cycles of the day and season, lest they all suffer for it.

He was bone weary and his clothes were damp with sweat when he returned to the kitchen door late in the afternoon. His scratches from the misadventure with the goat in the bramble, forgotten in the rush of more pressing concerns, were making themselves known with a vengeance. He wished he had more of the soothing ointment to apply, and missed the rejuvenating effects of his accustomed midday switchel. He hoped that he might be able to at least locate the bottle Constance kept that in before he turned to the chore of attempting supper.

He was surprised to find Mister Hillyard sitting at the kitchen table, a cup and a jug before him. Controlling the flash of anger that passed through him when he thought about the man's role in inviting his daughter's assailant into their home, Arthur turned to leave the farmer in peace.

Mister Hillyard called out, "Nay, come, sit, join me and take your ease for a moment. You've earned it, son."

Reluctantly, Arthur approached the table, and the older man motioned to the sideboard. "Get yourself a cup, if you like. There's some cider left yet."

Arthur did as Mister Hillyard suggested and sat opposite him at the table. He was shocked to see that the man seemed to have aged a decade overnight. The stubble of his unshaven face was white, and his jowls sagged as though his cheeks were too tired to hold them up. His unkempt hair only added to the impression of decrepitude, and as he shakily tipped the jug to pour the last of the cider into Arthur's cup, the younger man realized that Mister Hillyard was intoxicated.

"Thank you, sir," he murmured as his host set the empty jug back on the table with a deliberate thump.

"'Tis the least I could do," Mister Hillyard said, with a grim smile. "I'm glad someone's been attending to his duties around this place."

Arthur stopped with his cup halfway to his mouth and started to object, but Mister Hillyard raised a hand to indicate that he would brook no argument. "Nay, if I had done mine, that boy would never have crossed this threshold, and I would not have let my hope for a greater legacy for my daughter instead lead to her assault at his hands."

He scowled as he recalled, "I've known his father since they earned their grant and built their house. Jack was always a proud boy, taking after his father's haughtiness at having secured a better holding than most any in the district. Mister Contant believed that his good fortune proved that the Lord himself favored him over the rest of us."

Mister Hillyard shook his head, his eyes on some distant object that only he could see. "I thought the boy could overcome his father's weaknesses, and prove his worth on his own merits. As we have now seen, I was wrong in that, wrong about his ability to honestly win my daughter's heart . . . and wrong to trust him with her honor."

He lifted his cup to his lips, and seemed puzzled to find it empty. Frowning, he set the cup down and grimaced. "As it is, both my wife and my daughter blame me for what happened, and I can offer no argument to the contrary. There is no excuse for putting my ambitions ahead of their happiness, and it is an error which I will regret to the end of my days."

Arthur dared to speak then. "Mister Hillyard, if I may offer my view of having but a few months' experience of your household?

Your daughter holds you in high esteem, and with good cause. She was willing to entertain this boy out of her regard for you, and it is in no part your failure that he turned out to be unworthy of your trust or hers. That is *his* failure, and one which I warrant you will find a way to give him cause to repent in good time, if you've not already done so."

The farmer nodded blearily at Arthur, and then slammed his fist down suddenly on the table, making the cups dance upon it noisily. "Oh, yes, that I shall. I missed him in the night, but I will make him regret that he ever laid eyes on my Constance, let alone his filthy hands."

Chapter 8

Leaving Mister Hillyard snoring gently on the table where he'd said he would rest his head "only for a moment, and then I'll be right again," Arthur brought the tray with two plates upon it up the stairs. As well as bringing the dishes down from Constance's room, he noted that someone had righted the settee, though it still had the look of being somehow out of place.

At the top of the stairs, he called out, "I've a supper here, if you would eat."

Missus Hillyard replied, "Bring it in. Constance and I were just talking."

He carried the try in and set it down again on Constance's writing desk, and then turned to face the women. Constance sat up now, the eye on the bruised side of her face still somewhat swollen, but she looked substantially more alert than she had in the morning.

Her eyes were rimmed in red, as though she'd spent most of the day crying, but when she looked at Arthur, he could see her make the effort to hold her head high, and to regard him steadily. Her hair was loose and uncovered, and it occurred to him that he'd never thought about how long it was before.

"Good afternoon, Mister Leary," she said quietly. "I trust that my Papa has already taken his meal?"

Arthur hesitated. "Mister Hillyard... is indisposed at the moment."

Missus Hillyard, who'd been looking at Arthur as steadily as had her daughter, looked down suddenly, a pinched expression on her face. She looked back up and said, "Thank you, Mister Leary."

"You are welcome, of course. I have only done what is decent and right. Supper is nothing fancy, as I truly have no particular skill at the hearth, but I hope that it is edible, at least." He carried their plates to them, and reached back to the tray to retrieve spoons.

"I will take my leave and retire to my quarters for the evening. I hope that you rest well." He caught Constance's eye, and she nodded just perceptibly.

"A restful night to you, too," she said, and took a bit of the stew he'd made. He left the room, impressed that she had not made a face, as he was keenly aware that he'd been too free with the salt, and though he'd boiled the potted beef, it still retained its fibrous texture. He seemed to remember that Jameson had always said that it required nearly a full day of boiling to be soft, but there had been no time for that, nor anyone to tend to it while he was taking care of the chores all about the farm.

He returned to the kitchen to gather his plate, and to check on Mister Hillyard. The man had not moved since Arthur had left him, and was still snoring lightly into his arm. Arthur shook his head sadly at the man's state, but left him undisturbed, closing the door behind himself as he carried his dinner to the barn.

After just a few bites of his stew, he concluded that "edible" might be stretching the point, but he'd certainly had worse cooking than this, and the day's labors had left him hungry enough to eat boiled shoe leather, as he'd heard it said that the American army waiting to menace Philadelphia had done.

Sleep that night was again fitful due to the itching bramble scratches and a loud and lengthy fight outside his door between two cats, but it was, blessedly, not interrupted again by a human disturbance in the night.

In the morning, he awoke to Missus Hillyard, who brought in his breakfast as though nothing were out of the ordinary, though she did not linger to gossip, and indeed said nothing but a quiet, "Good morning" as she set down his bowl and hurried out.

Mister Hillyard, it appeared, was still indisposed, but Arthur had enough of a sense of the routines of the farm to carry on without instruction for several days, so he set about doing what he knew needed doing. The barn should be swept, lest it become fouled, and though he did not relish another episode with the goat — George, he reminded himself, as willful as the American general after whom Constance had told him with a grin that the beast had been named — he set about the task, applying more care to ensuring that the creature was kept under control.

The care of the animals' pens complete, he left them out to forage in their paddocks as he'd seen Constance do, while he spent the rest of the morning weeding in the field. The sun was high in the sky and he was sweating freely when Constance herself emerged from the kitchen door, bearing two tin cups, just as though her eye were not blacked and the events of the prior day were to be forgotten.

He met her at the stone fence, under the shade of their favorite tree, and accepted the cup she offered. Her expression was somber, but hardly the stricken face of terror and trauma he'd seen the prior day.

"Papa is feeling unwell today, but he asked me to convey his gratitude, as well. Our family is lucky to have you in our service, Mister Leary."

"Call me Arthur," he said suddenly, though he was not even sure what prompted it.

She took a sip of her switchel and he could see that she smiled, just barely, into her cup. "Very well, Arthur. You should use my familiar name, as well, as I find that your station in life and mine are not so far apart as we might have once supposed."

He nodded, feeling somehow that bringing her a smile was reason enough for him to have spoken up.

He did not like the thought that she felt her station lowered by the actions of a vile man, but could think of no way to object on those grounds without violating the delicate pretense of normality that she was clearly trying to hold together.

"'Tis warm today," he offered. "But it looks as though a storm may break later." The towering clouds gathering on the horizon promised a wild afternoon and evening, and he resolved to return the animals to their stalls before finishing the weeding.

He drained his cup, looking to the horizon with a mixture of fear and nostalgia.

The sight made him think of the storms that he'd seen sweep over the landscape back home, coming over the hills like an invading army, and he suddenly felt an overpowering pang of yearning for the distant land of England.

Of course, there, a storm like this could be seen gathering its strength over the hills for hours before it might reach his home, and there was little shelter out-of-doors either.

Here, at least, the woods crowded close around nearly all of the verges of what fields had been cleared.

He was so caught up in the memory of home that he almost missed her quiet reply. "Aye, the weather can change in an instant, like anything else."

He looked back to her bruised face, finding her lost in sad thought, her gaze stuck on some meaningless detail on the bark of the tree in whose shade they stood. There seemed no way to pierce the veil of sadness that he could see in her expression, so rather than trying to find the right thing to say, he just sat in silence with her, letting his own gaze slide down to the trunk of the tree.

Finally, she spoke, reaching out and laying her hand on the tree, her graceful fingers splayed across the rough bark. "I have loved this tree ever since I was little. It seemed as though it had always been here, and would always be."

Arthur looked up from her hand to her eyes, which were still fixed on the tree.

"When Papa cleared this field, he planned to extend it all the way to the entrance of the road, and I heard him tell Mama that he was planning to cut down this tree. I begged him to spare it, told him that I would do anything if only he would leave this dear old tree to live its days out in peace."

She looked up at Arthur then, her mouth curving into a gentle, wan smile. "Papa made me no promises, and extracted none from me, but when he put aside the plow for the day, he had shortened the field by enough to accommodate the tree. He never spoke of it, but only slowly built up the fence around it, marking for all time the boundary of his field."

She glanced up into the leafy crown of the old maple. "I

used to climb up nearly to the top of my tree, as high as the branches could bear my weight, even though Papa said that it wasn't right for a little girl to do so. But I could see so far from the top, looking down onto the roof of the house and even the barn, and it gave me such a thrill."

She looked down again, her smile fading and the earlier sadness reappearing. "Then, one day after a rain, I was climbing as usual, and I lost my grip on a wet branch. I was only saved from falling all the way to the ground by a limb catching me in the ribs. Though I was glad to be spared a worse injury, it left me stiff and sore whenever I drew too deep a breath for a month after."

Glancing up at Arthur from under her lashes, she concluded, "When I say that anything can change in an instant, that's what I think of. I felt like my tree, which I had trusted to lift and hold me a hundred feet in the air, had betrayed me that day, and I never, ever climbed it again."

She finished her cup and reached for his empty one. He handed it to her, mumbling his thanks, and she returned to the house.

A short time later, as he was escorting George and the rest of the animals back into the barn, he was reminded of his encounter with the brambles. Almost as soon as he thought of them, he wished he hadn't, because every scratch and scrape started itching.

He tried to ignore it as he returned to his weeding, for he knew that scratching at the itches would only re-open the cuts, but merely telling himself to think of something else only focused his mind on it all the more. Worse, one of the areas that itched the most was in the middle of his back, where he could not possibly reach it.

By the time the first heavy drops of rain sent him running for the barn, even just the texture of his shirt was nearly enough to drive him half-mad.

Once in his quarters, he pulled it off and stretched it between his hands so that he could draw it back and forth across his back to give him some relief.

Sitting down on his stool, he breathed slowly and deliberately, trying to relax and think of what he could do to rid himself of the itch. Perhaps Missus Hillyard knew how to mix up a ointment for that? He resolved to go to the kitchen door and ask, as soon as the rain let up.

Just then, he heard what sounded like a stall door in the barn banging against the wall, and he froze. Had he failed to secure the doors properly? Or was there some intruder with him in the barn?

He hurriedly pulled his damp shirt back over his head and went out to investigate.

It was dark in the barn, with the storm picking up in intensity, and the noise of the raindrops on the roof was nearly deafening. But even in the limited light, he could see that one of the stalls was standing wide open.

He moved closer to see whether the old cow that normally occupied it was still within, or if she had somehow kicked the door open and escaped.

He was still trying to remember whether he'd secured it properly when he saw that the cow was standing quietly in the far end of the stall, chewing her cud. However, there was a small figure moving about in front of her. Arthur moved deeper into the darkness of the stall and asked, "Who is there?"

An ear-piercing shriek rent the air, and Constance leapt upward, nearly colliding with the cow. Arthur put his hands on her shoulders to steady her, and she shrieked again, turning to face him and beating his chest with her fists, wailing and struggling.

He hurriedly released her shoulders and stepped back, dumbstruck but giving her room to burst past him and dash out of the barn and into the storm toward the house.

Chapter 9

Arthur stood outside the kitchen door, waiting in the rain for someone to come in answer to his knock. He was just about to give up and return to his quarters when Missus Hillyard opened the door, her face nearly as stormy as the skies as she looked him up and down.

"What do you mean by sneaking up behind my Constance in the barn, with your shirt all untucked, and grabbing her out of the darkness?"

Arthur's mouth dropped open for a moment before he could gather his wits enough to answer. "I did not know it was her in the barn. I was only trying to learn whether it was an intruder of some sort." He looked down to see that his shirt-tails were, indeed, out of his breeches, and added, "My shirt is untucked because I was trying to scratch the places on my back where I was hurt in the brambles."

Missus Hillyard's expression softened by degrees as she considered his explanation. Finally, she *tsked* at him, shaking her head. "I knew it had to have been some sort of misunderstanding, as that seemed well outside of your character. Well, come in out of the storm, then, and we'll get you dried off, and see what we can do for your wounds."

He entered through the door she held open for him and as she closed it behind him, she said, "Let's get that wet shirt off of you and sit you down before the fire to warm up and dry off."

He did as she said, picking up a chair and setting it before the hearth before pulling his shirt off over his head and placing it in her outstretched hand. She draped it over the back of another chair and moved behind him to examine his back.

She clucked her tongue again in disapproval as she looked at the scratches on his back. "You've gotten all inflamed, what with the neglect and hard work of the past few days. I'll need to prepare another ointment for you to take some of the heat out of your skin, and to soothe your itching."

He slumped into the chair. "I had intended to come and ask whether you might be able to do that, before I . . . frightened Miss Hillyard. Thank you very kindly."

"Of course," she said, an edge of crispness in her tone. "With all you've done for us these past days, I am happy to do this little thing for you."

He sat and soaked in the warmth from the hearth as she moved about the kitchen, gathering and mixing various ingredients. Missus Hillyard described to Arthur what she was mixing together, and the importance of the techniques by which she had gathered and prepared and ground this and that. As she progressed into the details of how she was blending the different components, and in what sequence, the talk was well beyond Arthur's ken, and he found himself dozing off in the chair.

He only awoke when he heard Missus Hillyard say, "And so that's done now. I'll just apply it to your back, Mister Leary, and you'll be right in no time." She came around to examine his back, an earthenware pot in her hand.

Arthur could hear her moving around behind him, and even

so hissed in surprise as the cold of the ointment first touched his skin. He willed himself to hold still, though, and he could feel her practiced hands spreading it over his scrapes, and then working it into his skin. Whatever was in the ointment stung as it found broken skin, but that faded quickly enough, leaving behind only a chill, despite the warmth of the hearth.

"Many's the time I've had to make the like of this for Mister Hillyard," she remarked, as she started in on the scratches on his shoulders and arms. "You've put up much less fuss than he usually does. Did I make it wrong, or does it not string like salt in a cut?"

He managed to chuckle, and answered, "Oh, aye, it stings perfectly well, don't you worry about that. Somewhat less than the first ointment, but I have no doubt as to the effect of either one."

He glanced out the window, noticing that the storm seemed to be abating. "Strange that we had such a terrific downpour and no thunder. A great gully-washer like that back home would have had old Thor banging about like a party."

He could just see Missus Hillyard's smile out of the corner of his eye. "Oh, we have our share of thunder and lightning in these parts, as well. I'm glad enough for the rain, though, without a lot of wind or hail, as I believe that the crops are yet fairly delicate, from what Mister Hillyard's said."

"Hail would do them no good, it's true, but most everything is far enough along now to be able to stand up to a bit of wind and a downpour. I'm just glad for the break from the heat."

She made a knowing gesture with her head and said, "The heat of the summer's barely risen yet. We'll have plenty of days yet that will make you yearn for this early season."

He grimaced, but said nothing. She moved around to his

other side and worked the ointment into one particularly vicious set of scratches — Arthur seemed to remember that the goat had deliberately dragged that arm through a dense part of the bramble — and the stinging there made him swallow some choice curses.

Aloud, and through clenched teeth, he said only, "Oh, yes, I can assure you that your ointment is as effective as ever, Missus Hillyard."

She smiled without mirth and finished working the ointment into his skin. When she was done, she set the pot down on the side table and put a plate over it to cover it. "There's enough left for another dose in the morning, which should be sufficient to make you right again. Come in and see me after you break your fast, and I'll apply it where you can't reach."

He stood and retrieved his shirt, now significantly dryer than when he'd come in, and pulled it over his head. "Might I make my apologies to Miss Hillyard before I return to my work for the afternoon?"

Missus Hillyard shook her head firmly. "Nay, there's no use. When she came in, she could barely speak, she had such a fright of you, and she went right up to her room. Closed it fast behind her, too. Better to wait until the morning, and we will see whether she has recovered herself sufficiently."

Arthur's head dropped, and he grimaced. "Very well. If there is aught that I can do before then to help her, please fetch me."

He thought he saw a glimmer of compassion in her eyes, but she only nodded briskly. "Aye, that I will." She turned to get started on supper, and he returned to the field to finish the weeding.

He supposed that he must have been consumed with the work at hand, because he didn't even see that Mister Hillyard had left until the man came stomping back down the road, his curled fist held to his mouth.

The farmer's stormy expression cleared substantially when he saw Arthur stand up fully from where he'd been pulling weeds. The older man wiped his fist on his breeches, leaving a bloody streak, and strode over to the fencerow at the edge of the field.

"If you should see that young Mister Contant skulking about — you'll know him by his broken face — I give you leave to practice the arts of violence upon him in any way that might suit you."

Arthur cocked a brow at Mister Hillyard and replied, "I've few such arts that are useful without my Brown Bess, but you have my word that I will improvise as best I can, should I spy him."

He motioned at the stone fence. "I have some ideas that might involve dislodging couple of those rocks for a higher purpose. I reckon I can throw with a decent degree of accuracy, if I should spot him from afar." He shrugged. "If not, the hoe will serve in an alternate use well enough."

The farmer gave him a wicked grin and slapped his own knee before going on into the house. Arthur was glad to see that Mister Hillyard was in better spirits, and was further satisfied that the target of his rage deserved every bit of the beating that it sounded as if he had received, and then some. It was positively healing for a man to have some action that he could take to put things right, if only by a little.

On reflection, Arthur was pleased that Mister Hillyard had been occupied with dispensing some justice when he'd surprised

Constance in the barn, else he might have been the object of such action himself, before their misunderstanding could have been resolved.

    The sun's slow descent toward the horizon gave him cause enough to gather up the weeds he had pulled into his apron and trudge back to the barn to toss them to the goats, before sitting down to await his supper.

Chapter 10

Arthur presented himself to Missus Hillyard at the kitchen door, his empty breakfast plate and bowl in his hand. "The ointment worked a treat last night," he said as she took the dishes from him. "I am not even sure that I need another dose today."

She fixed him with a frown and said, "None of that, my boy. You'll sit and take your medicine like a man, and let it finish its work on you."

He let his shoulders slump and said, "Very well. I only hope that it does not burn so much today."

"Well, if it has healed you so much as you say it has, then it should scarcely prick at all. Go hang your shirt on a chair, and sit as you did yesterday."

He meekly did as he was told, and waited before the fire as Missus Hillyard gathered up the earthenware pot and started toward him, her eyes fixed on him with a determined expression on her face.

He did not hear Constance enter the kitchen, so he startled slightly when he heard her soft voice from the doorway behind him. "Mister Leary, I owe you an apology, I think."

He twisted in the chair to see her looking very small and forlorn, holding the door frame as though for strength. The bruise around her eye was still deeply purpled at its core, but was starting to fade to a garish yellow at one edge. He tore his gaze away from it and said, "It was I who surprised you, Miss Hillyard," taking his cue from her formal use of his surname instead of his familiar name. "So it is I who owe you an apology."

She emerged fully from the door and shook her head. "Nay, you had no way of knowing I was in the barn, and every reason to come and investigate whatever noise I was making." She wrung her hands and bit her lip before continuing.

"It was only that finding you so close behind me, and without knowing that you were there at all, I was reminded most forcefully of . . . what happened the other night. When you tried to keep me from falling over, I lost my senses for a moment, and could think only of making my escape."

She then turned to Missus Hillyard. "Mama," she said, "I know that I must have frightened you, as well, and I am sorry for that. Once I regained my senses, I knew at once what had happened, and I felt ashamed for having worried everyone." She smiled slightly, adding, "At least Papa was still abroad and was not disturbed by my fit."

Missus Hillyard set down the ointment pot and bustled across the room to envelop Constance in an embrace. "Oh, my child," she murmured into her daughter's hair, "You've nothing to feel shame about, nothing whatever."

She released her daughter and motioned her to another chair at the table. "Sit, while I finish with Mister Leary's new ointment. His scrapes still need at least one more dose."

Constance got up from the table and approached Arthur, peering at his back and shoulders, her eyes traveling over the places where his skin had torn while he struggled with the goat. She reached a hand out to her mother, saying quietly, "Let me."

Missus Hillyard said nothing, though one eyebrow rose of its own accord, and passed the container over to her daughter. "Mind that you rub it in well," she advised, and Constance nodded.

The first touch of the cold ointment was still a shock to Arthur's senses, and he inhaled sharply, but the sting was far more bearable today. He realized as she started to spread it across his back that her hands were shaking ever so slightly, and he hoped that she was not still afraid of him after yesterday's incident.

However, after a little while, her touch became more sure, and her small, strong hands worked the ointment into his wounds. He found that he barely minded how it hurt, even when Missus Hillyard brought Constance's attention to the places on his arm that bore the deepest scratches. He couldn't think of the last time he'd been touched with such care.

When she was finished, she stepped back and handed the pot with its remaining ointment back to her mother. Arthur smiled tentatively as he stood and pulled his shirt back on. "Thank you for your kind attention, Miss Hillyard."

She inclined her head and replied with an inscrutable expression, "You are welcome, Arthur. I hope that it doesn't bother you as you work today." She paused and added, "I will be sweeping out the barn today as usual, and I would appreciate it if you would announce yourself, should you happen to be within at the same time as I."

"Of course, Constance," he said. "I do not expect that my chores today will put me in your way at all, but I will take pains not to again surprise you."

Missus Hillyard gave them a quizzical look — Arthur

guessed due to their use of familiar names with one another in her presence — but said nothing, as he went out into the sunshine to start his morning duties.

Shortly afterward, Mister Hillyard joined him, flexing the fingers of the hand he'd bruised the day before and muttering under his breath. As he came into earshot, he said to Arthur, "If you'd not scratched yourself up on those brambles, Missus Hillyard would not have had that accursed ointment of hers at the ready for my hand." He shook his fingers in the air, and Arthur did his best to stifle a chuckle.

The farmer gazed at the fields thoughtfully for a moment and then looked Arthur over with an appraising eye. "Have you ever wielded a scythe?"

Arthur looked back at him with alarm. "Nay, my father always hired in haymakers for that work."

Mister Hillyard uttered a bark of laughter. "Well, we've no such luxury here. The hay's ready, so I'll teach you." He led Arthur to the barn and reached up to pull the long tool off the rafter where it was hung. Arthur kept his distance as Mister Hillyard brought it out into the sunlight, setting the end of the handle on the ground so they could easily see the blade at eye level.

The older man pulled a whetstone out of the pocket that he had tied at his waist, and held it up. "I trust you've experience with touching up a blade?"

"Aye," Arthur said. He did not mention that the last time he'd sharpened a knife, he had contrived somehow to shave off a thin, painful strip from the heel of his thumb. Unconsciously, his fingers traced the scar that misadventure had left him.

Mister Hillyard nodded briskly and examined the blade

of the scythe minutely. "I put this away clean, dry, and freshly sharpened and oiled, but after the damp of the winter, I'm sure it is no longer so keen. In any event, it never hurts to put a fresh edge on it before using it." He drew the whetstone evenly along the curved blade, which was easily the length of Arthur's arm.

Frowning, he repeated the motion on one side a few times, and even Arthur could hear the difference from one stroke to the next. He then ran the stone along the underside of the blade once, and twice. By the time Mister Hillyard was finished, the stone barely whispered along the metal, and left it faintly ringing when it cleared the pointed end.

"We'll need to freshen the edge as we go, but it's about as good as it will ever be now." He picked it up and rotated the blade to lie along the ground in front of him, gripping it with one hand high on the shaft of the handle, and the other on the short handle that projected from the shaft at a right angle, level with the ground.

"So. You will hold it like this, and start by pulling your arm back to open the cut." He demonstrated, the arm holding the top end of the shaft swinging back, bringing the tip of the blade out in front of him.

"It might feel like you ought to swing the whole thing before you wildly, but you will only damage the blade and tire yourself." He grinned, and continued, "You will cut less hay, and will ache all night for how little you've gotten done. No, instead, you will hold your left hand relatively still in relation to your body, and use the right hand to pivot the blade before you, like this."

He pushed the top of the handle forward smoothly across his body at hip height, and the blade swept over the ground in front of him. "I have been doing this since I was younger than you are now, so the motion is second nature to me now." He repeated it a few times, and Arthur observed him closely, frowning in concentration.

Mister Hillyard stopped and gestured for him to step back a bit. When Arthur was out of harm's way, he hoisted the blade up toward his shoulder and rested it there, point forward. "When you're carrying the scythe around, you may be tempted to put the blade over your shoulder, instead of pointing it forward. If you trip and fall with it that way, though, it will slice you to ribbons, whereas if I were to trip now, I would naturally throw the blade away from my body."

He smiled tightly and added, "'Tis better not to fall at all while you carry such a tool, however, lest you ruin the edge we've put on it, so watch your footing as you walk. Now, let me show you how the cut looks in the field."

Arthur dutifully followed Mister Hillyard out to the field, grown thigh-high. Still holding the scythe with the blade up, the farmer bent and swept his hand through the grass. "Perfect," he remarked, and then explained, "We want the grass still just barely damp from the morning dew in order to best cut it. With yesterday's rain, I much doubt that we will have any difficulty, but if the day turns hot, we will have to cut the work short."

He chuckled at his own witticism, and Arthur smiled politely, although his time on the Hillyard farm had not done much for his patience at puns.

The older man swung the scythe down from his shoulder, and positioned it as before. The blade swept forward, and a swath of grass fell before it, most of which was carried over to lie at the side of the space cleared. Mister Hillyard rocked back as he swung the blade to its original position, and then stepped forward a bit to start the next cut.

He repeated this several times before holding the implement out to Arthur. "Here, see if you can put this education to use."

Arthur took it from him with trepidation and attempted to mimic the positioning that he'd been shown. Mister Hillyard stepped forward at once and corrected his grip, and then stepped back.

"Good, show me how you would cut." Arthur gave the tool a tentative swing. "Hold the blade closer to the ground," the farmer called out, and added, "Good, good," as Arthur adjusted his swing.

"Remember, you're not waving a sword or a bayonet, but mowing. Your right hand should do most of the work." He continued giving Arthur encouragement and suggestions until he finally said, "Now, let's see how you do on the grass."

The first swath was a disaster, even Arthur could see as much. More than half of the blades of grass he'd tried to gather with the tip of the blade had only been knocked flat, and what he had cut was uneven and looked more ripped than sliced. Behind him, he heard Mister Hillyard say, "A shorter swath, and more speed."

Arthur rocked back as he'd seen the older man do, and stepped forward, sweeping the blade along the ground to re-cut the same grass, but in a narrower strip. Somewhat more satisfied with the results, he repeated the motion and heard Mister Hillyard grunt behind him, "You say you've never done this before?"

Arthur paused at the beginning of the next stroke and

stood upright. "Nay. Though I passed a day once watching the haymakers at their work. I never made brave enough to ask to handle their scythes, however." He pointed with his chin at the blade. "Anything that sharp and large frightened me excessively as a boy."

Mister Hillyard laughed heartily. "I suppose you had to get over that in order to sign up to be a soldier, though, eh?"

Arthur shrugged. "Private soldiers and other enlisted men don't have swords, and bayonets are somehow less frightening, for all that they are probably deadlier than this thing would be in combat. Each instrument has its own purpose, and it only unnerved me before I understood that properly."

The farmer grimaced at Arthur's frank assessment. "You seem to have the feel of that, at least," he nodded toward the scythe. "Let's have you work down the row here, and see how you feel when you're done. If you've got it right, you shouldn't be all that fatigued, but if you are, where you're hurting will tell us what we need to improve in your form."

Arthur nodded and went to work, the blade whispering through the grass as it fell before him. More often than he would like, he repeated the same mistakes of the first stroke, and had to remind himself that less grass under the blade would cut more, and more speed would cut better.

When he reached the end of the field, where Mister Hillyard was waiting for him, he straightened and leaned his weight on the handle of the scythe, kneading the small of his back with his free hand.

Mister Hillyard smiled at him.

"Do you suppose you know what you need to do differently

in order for your back not to hurt?"

Arthur frowned at him, and answered, "Let my arms do more of the work, and my back less?"

"Aye — indeed, your back ought to do almost none of it. Don't be too disappointed with yourself, though. When I was first learning how to use the scythe, I was so back-sore that I could scarcely move for a week."

He smiled gently in reminiscence, and Arthur was struck suddenly by the odd image of Mister Hillyard as a youth, years from being the seemingly all-knowing, all-capable man he knew.

The man's smile gradually faded, though, and he pointed down the next side of the field. "We'll work our way around the field, so that the cut grass may fall onto bare ground as we go. This row, put your mind to making the swathe as neat and uniform as ever you can. It will make for less effort with the hay-rake when we are finished with the mowing."

Arthur nodded and set to it. The rhythm of the blade was almost relaxing, for all that it was hard labor. Its path through the stalks of grass made a susurration that was different in quality from the sound of a body merely moving through a field. Rather than being pushed aside and then springing back, the grass was falling to the ground, and that sequence of events had its own music to it.

His mind drifted through these thoughts as his body labored, and before he knew it, he was done with the second side of the field. Mister Hillyard was there again. "Did that feel better?"

"Oh, aye," replied Arthur immediately. "I barely felt the strain down this swathe."

"Good," Mister Hillyard nodded. "When you've finished a circuit, I will spell you for the next, and then we'll switch back, and so on until the grass is too dry, or we've finished the job."

Arthur continued mowing as directed, and the repetitive sweep of his arms reminded him somehow of the repetitive motions of marching, and he settled into the same sort of mindless routine he remembered finding himself in during his army training back home.

When he reached the end of his first circuit around the field, he handed the scythe over to Mister Hillyard, who said, "Go and get us two large cups of switchel. It was made for this kind of work, and will help sustain you for as long as we can continue at it."

Arthur nodded and went to house, and into the kitchen, where Missus Hillyard and Constance were sitting and peeling potatoes for their supper.

Missus Hillyard looked up as he entered. "Mister Hillyard sent you in to fetch some switchel, I'll warrant?"

"Aye," Arthur answered. "He asked for a large cup for the both of us."

At a glance from Missus Hillyard, Constance set down her knife and the potato she was working on and sprang up to pour him two cups.

She had to tilt the jug up nearly vertical to fill the second cup, and she said to her mother, "We shall have to make up a fresh jug right away. Papa will want more soon."

Missus Hillyard shook her head and said, "Well, you know where the vinegar and molasses are. I don't know if we have any ginger left, but we can make it plain, if not. 'Tis just as sustaining without it, if not quite as refreshing."

"Oh, no, we still have ginger. It's in a sack in the pantry." She gestured at a small door on the far side of hearth. Arthur frowned to himself at not having discovered the pantry when he was trying to cook. Doubtless, that was where the molasses he'd sought was kept, too.

"You go ahead and get that started, then," Missus Hillyard said. "I'll finish the potatoes on my own."

Constance smiled at him and handed him the two cups. "I will bring a fresh jug out when I have it ready, Arthur."

He smiled back, accepting the cups. "I thank you very kindly, Constance. I am quite certain your father appreciates it as well."

She tilted her head in acknowledgment, and he brought the cups outside.

He came to a stop, leaning against the shade tree and watched Mister Hillyard make quick work of what remained of his circuit. The man's swathe was even and smooth, and the row of felled grass formed a tidy line beside it.

He studied Mister Hillyard's form to see how it differed from his own, and decided that for the most part, it must be in small details that he supposed would become second nature to him over time, just as they had for the older man.

He took a deep draught of the switchel and was amazed at how delicious it tasted today. He supposed that it must contain just exactly what his sore muscles were craving, given that he felt better when he finished his cup than he had before picking up the scythe to begin with.

When he saw that Mister Hillyard was approaching the end of his circuit, he set his empty cup beside the tree and walked out to the field to hand the farmer his share of the elixir, and to take the scythe from him. Mister Hillyard accepted the cup from him, and drained it in one go, smacking his lips when he was finished.

"Nothing better on mowing day," he declared, and Arthur could make no argument. Mister Hillyard then took Arthur's place under the shade tree, and Arthur bent to starting his next circuit of the field.

Constance must have been watching through the window, for she was out with the jug as Arthur was just mowing the last strip. She filled her father's cup, and he again drained it at a single pull, before going back out to the field with the scythe, which Arthur had handed over to him.

In the sunlight, Arthur could see that the bruise under Constance's eye had developed a greenish tinge around one side, and his fists clenched involuntarily at the sight. He found himself hoping that young Mister Contant would make an appearance, so he could have a turn at the scoundrel.

The ugliness of the bruise disappeared, though, when Constance smiled at him as she poured him a cup of the freshly-made switchel. He felt almost as though the sun had emerged from behind a cloud, even though there wasn't a single cloud in the midmorning sky.

He smiled back with easy camaraderie as he sipped from the cup. The ginger in the fresh switchel was a little sharper than in the older batch, but that only made it all the more refreshing, in his opinion.

"Thank you, most kindly, for making up more to keep us going at this," he said. She smiled again, dimpling her cheeks, then set the jug down beside the tree, and went back inside without having said a word.

He finished his cup and sat down under the tree to wait for

his next circuit. While his upper arm was starting to feel sore from the endless cycle of sweeping back and forth, the drink still made him feel ready to return to the field when it was his turn.

He and Mister Hillyard switched off in this manner as the morning stretched into afternoon. When the farmer finished the last circuit of the field, he returned to the tree and drank the last of the switchel directly from the jug. He belched gently and said, "I was worried that we would not finish before the grass grew too dry to cut. We've done well, and you are welcome to rest until supper."

Arthur rose wearily from where he sat, with his back against the tree. "Thank you, Mister Hillyard. I shall have a keener appreciation of the work of the haymakers now. I also understand better how they could sleep through nearly anything when they finished for the day."

The older man smiled indulgently at him. "Tomorrow, we rake the swathes into even rows, that they may turn more evenly as they dry."

Arthur stifled a groan, and the farmer added, "You are welcome to dine indoors with us today, if you like."

Arthur nodded. "I would like that very well, and I thank you for the invitation. I will bathe and change before supper."

The older man laughed aloud, and said, "As will I, lest Missus Hillyard should make me eat out in the barn with you."

Chapter II

Arthur was coming to appreciate, in a way he never had as a child, that farming was one endless set of tasks after another, each competing for which would be the most arduous. Mowing hay was hard work, but raking it seemed like punishment for some sin of a past life. Over and over again, Mister Hillyard showed him the careful sequence of motions necessary to straighten the row and turn it so that its wet underside was exposed to the heat of the sun. And over and over again, the subtleties of this task seemed to escape Arthur.

Again fortified with a fresh jug of switchel — Missus Hillyard had made one along with their breakfast — the men got through the work, but they spent most of the day frustrated with one another. Arthur could honestly see no discernible difference between his row and the one that Mister Hillyard had laid out next to it, and yet the farmer found fault every single time. They sniped back and forth, neither of them seemingly able to understand what the other was getting at.

To make matters worse, the motion of raking hay was not a natural, balanced sequence like that of mowing. By the time the sun grew low in the sky, the field was no more than half raked, and Arthur's shoulders felt as though they had been pummeled all day. He was eager for dinner and the sweet release of sleep.

As they trudged out of the field side by side, Mister Hillyard grunted, "Tomorrow, you'll weed, and I will do the raking. I hope that you will pardon me for being so particular all day. My sleep last night was interrupted by my daughter waking up shouting from a nightmare, and I was enraged anew at Mister Contant's presumption. It was not right, however, for me to mistreat you in my anger at someone else."

The irritation that Arthur had felt building up all day dissipated in an instant. "Is Constance all right?"

Mister Hillyard grimaced. "It will be some time before she is anything close to all right, but she is at least persevering. She is stronger than she knows, even if it may take her a while to come to that understanding herself."

Arthur said nothing, but his heart ached for the pain that Constance was enduring. He wished in vain that there were some way for him to demonstrate to her that some men could be trusted — that *he* could be trusted — despite her bitter experience.

The older man peered over at Arthur, and almost as though he could read the farmhand's thoughts, he said, "Worry not, my young friend. She'll learn to trust again, when she meets somebody who earns that honor." He sighed and added, "You're welcome to join us again for supper, if you're not weary of my company."

Arthur smiled at Mister Hillyard. "Nay, not weary of your company, just of the work. I will happily return to the weeding tomorrow — and I will be most grateful to sup in your company this evening."

In the pond as he washed himself and his clothing, he wondered at the farmer's comment about Constance finding someone whom she could trust. Was Mister Hillyard now hoping that Arthur would take the place of Constance's prior, disgraced suitor? Had he forgotten that they were on opposite sides of a war, and that Arthur was little more than a servant in their home?

For that matter, had Arthur himself lost track of that fact?

This family, like most everyone he had encountered in his travels through New-England, was deeply disloyal to the King, and dedicated to the cause of splitting these colonies away from the Crown. Could he truly call himself a friend to someone whose loyalties he did not share?

However, the kindnesses and confidences between himself and the Hillyard family seemed to transcend their political differences. Seeing how they lived here, how hard they all labored for what they had, he could even develop a faint understanding of how they might hold resentment toward a distant and meddlesome Parliament and King... and how they might have come to believe that their situation would be improved for leaving both behind.

However, he'd known from birth that he was a subject of the Crown, and that recourse to any local excesses of the King's representatives ought be addressed through the Parliament, and never, under even the most extreme imaginable circumstances, through taking up arms and revolting against the government. Aside from the self-evident uselessness of such an undertaking — imagine challenging the representatives of the most powerful nation in the world! — the disloyalty it exhibited to a nation that had provided protection and order was simply unthinkable.

As he finished bathing and washing and moved on to dressing, he concluded that he need not interrupt his friendship with these people, who had become something like a family to him. He remembered that he'd once heard a group of officers speaking amongst themselves in familiar and admiring terms of French officers of their acquaintance, and it had not interfered with their determination to defeat their friends on the field of battle, even if one or another should fall. Still, he expected that he would likely never fully understand the Hillyards' point of view.

As he walked toward the barn to finish readying himself for supper, he saw a horse and rider approaching on the road.

He froze, wondering if this was the infamous Mister Contant. His pulse quickened, and he cast about, looking for a rock or some other implement with which to punish Constance's tormentor, should this turn out to be him.

As he drew closer, though, he could see that the rider wore a neatly turned-out but otherwise modest cocked hat, and the rest of his appearance was similarly simply prosperous, where Contant's had been dandy. Further, his face was not broken in a manner to match Mister Hillyard's battered knuckles, and his hair was as neatly clubbed at his neck as was Arthur's own.

As the rider turned down toward the house, he called out, "Post rider, bearing a letter for a British prisoner out on labor contract, by the name of Leary!" He waved a folded letter by way of illustration, and Arthur stepped forward, frowning.

"That would be me," he said, moving in the direction of the horse and its rider.

The rider held the letter back, saying, "My instructions for this manner of post are to deliver it to the master of the house, who will see to its disposition." He glanced back at the letter and asked, "Is Mister Hillyard about?"

A flash of irritation ran across Arthur's face, but he nodded. "Aye, he's in the house. I'll go and call for him."

The post rider nodded at him, and Arthur turned to go

and knock at the kitchen door. Missus Hillyard came to the door, looking a bit flustered. "Supper's not quite ready yet, Mister Leary, though you're welcome to come in and wait at the table, if you like."

"What? Oh, no, I'm here to summon Mister Hillyard for a post rider, bearing a letter addressed to me. Apparently, he can only release the post to the master of the house, and not to the addressee." Arthur could hear that he was failing to keep his irritation out of his tone, but Missus Hillyard only nodded sympathetically.

"Oh, then, I'll go and fetch him. He should be finished dressing after cleaning himself up for supper."

She bustled off, leaving Arthur there at the door.

Inside, Constance was stirring a pot hanging over the fire, and she smiled at him, which helped to reduce his irritation somewhat. He smiled back, and then turned his attention outside once more, to the post rider.

The man had dismounted, and was examining his horse's hooves while he waited.

Arthur supposed that his work was relatively arduous and could even be dangerous, were he called to pass through the lines between rebel-held territory and that under the control of the King's loyal men. Still, the imperious manner with which he'd addressed Arthur rankled, and he retained a small coal of resentment in his heart toward the rider.

Mister Hillyard came downstairs and strolled out to greet the post rider, who immediately handed over Arthur's letter. They exchanged a few words, their tone sounding friendly to Arthur, though he could not make out what was being said. Then the post rider swung back into his saddle and wheeled his horse about to return to the road.

Mister Hillyard ambled back to the house, and held up the letter to hand it to Arthur as he approached.

"They have their rules, as does any service," he said, putting the letter into Arthur's outstretched hand. "I am sure you can appreciate that there could be circumstances under which the master might like to review correspondence before delivering its contents to someone in your position, but those circumstances do not obtain between you and I, of course. I trust that you will inform me of anything of import."

Arthur accepted the letter, nodding. "Of course, Mister Hillyard. Even though I can comprehend the necessity, it still sits poorly, as I am sure *you* can appreciate."

"I do understand. I'll see you at supper."

Arthur turned and walked toward the barn, examining the letter. He recognized the strong and untidy hand on the address as belonging to one of his men, Miller by name. That put him immediately at ease that it was not ill news from home, at least. The seal had been broken and a new one applied, and he guessed that it had had to pass American censors on its way to him.

He slid his finger under the new seal, breaking it and opened the letter as he entered the barn. He stopped at the door for the light there, and what he read elicited an involuntary gasp and nearly moved him to tears on the spot.

Jameson, his wife, and their new baby had all succumbed to a camp fever that had swept through the barracks a few weeks back.

Miller laid out the facts in spare, unadorned prose.

"*First he was taken ill, and nobody could physick him in*

the slightest, save for his devoted wife. He died the day before she was taken ill & along with her the baby.

"Though the American colonel was so moved by their plight to offer that a doctor be called, our lieutenant refused on grounds that they had refused to aid her husband, and he thought that a soldier's life ought be held in the same regard as any follower of the camp.

"In the end, the entire Jameson family was buried in a common grave, and now pass into eternity under American soil. Many more were taken from these barracks in the same way, but of our squad, only Jameson and his family were lost."

Staggering, Arthur went into his quarters and sat heavily on his stool. Jameson, who'd been so attached to his wife that he had brought her here with him across the sea. Jameson, whose baby's birth on the terrible passage from Saratoga to Cambridge had brought a little moment of joy in the midst of that horror. Gone, all of them . . . in a single blow, and even when their captors had been moved to compassion, British pride had rejected any assistance for the woman and baby.

Arthur felt a rage at his lieutenant then, beyond anything he could put words to. It was a matter of good fortune that he was here, and not there, because he was quite certain that he would have acted in a manner that would have earned him a trip to the post for a lashing — or even to the gallows to dance in a noose.

He tried to master himself, putting a hand on the sturdy table beside him, and reminding himself that the Jameson family was beyond his help now.

Of course, such a terrible circumstance might arise another time, and he wondered whether the lieutenant was so unfeeling a brute as to let a second family be destroyed completely under his orders.

Yet, what was the point of coming here and spilling British blood for the maintenance of order and law, if a man's family could be swept away in order to avoid giving the appearance of preferential treatment? Was it not a part of their charge in being here to protect the weak, and prevent them from suffering and dying? Why, if Arthur had been enraged by the violation of Miss Hillyard's innocence, how much more terrible a violation was it to let a woman and her baby die when an offer of help was at hand?

Arthur again took a slow, steadying breath, while his knuckles ached from the strain of gripping the table so tightly.

He had a flash of insight that felt as real and palpable as the tumbler of a lock falling into place to reveal what it secured. Disorder and death could come from any direction. It was not the exclusive province of either those who rebelled against the former order, nor of those who sought to maintain the status quo.

One could sow the seeds of destruction even while trying to do what seemed like the right thing. Even the most well-meaning action could result in disaster.

So how was one to ever act, knowing that the outcome could be anything but what was intended? Indeed, inaction could lead to disaster, so even that choice could not be proper, to one who wanted to avoid harm to others.

Arthur could dimly remember that his schoolmaster had spoken of the ancient philosophers having wrestled with similar questions, and he wished now that he had paid closer attention to that lesson than to the antics of his friends. He would have welcomed guidance even from men long since gone from the Earth, if only to offer some reassurance of what proper action might be.

If there was so little certainty that one's actions were correct, then what was the meaning of loyalty to a cause that might be as wrong as the one it opposed? What was the point of loyalty if it could cost you everything that was dearest to you — including your own life? Was not friendship, shared purpose, and shared sacrifice more meaningful?

Arthur was interrupted in this train of thought by Constance, who came and knocked at the door of his quarters.

"Are you coming to supper?" she asked.

He hurriedly wiped his nose on his sleeve and folded the letter to tuck it away under his pillow. He emerged into the barn to find Constance waiting for him at the door. When she saw him, she cried out, "Whatever is the matter, Arthur?"

Arthur bit his lower lip, hard, to control the tears that sought to well up again as he answered, "I have just received word that one of the men I commanded was lost to a camp fever, along with his wife and the baby whose birth I assisted in as we marched from Saratoga this winter past. 'Tis a heavy blow to bear."

He broke off as the tears got the better of him again, and Constance hurried across the few steps between them and gathered him into her arms. He returned her embrace as though it were the most natural and familiar thing in the world, and not the first time that he had really touched her at all.

When they finally released one another, he could see that her eyes, too, were bright with unshed tears. He pulled her into another embrace, and when they finally parted to go inside for supper, they found Missus Hillyard giving them an appraising look at the kitchen door.

She said nothing, though Arthur thought he caught a glimpse of a smile before she turned and went inside.

Chapter 12

Missus Hillyard hadn't been wrong when she had said that the heat of the summer was yet to come. Arthur wiped away a trickle of sweat that threatened to course into his eye, where he knew it would sting and blind him. And he needed his eyes for the mindless, back-breaking work of picking beetles off of the squash.

Mister Hillyard had shown him the squash patch, instructing him, "Mind that you don't step on the stems or break off the immature fruits as you go."

Seeing Arthur's dismay at the dense tangle of stems that he'd have to pick through, he added contemplatively, "I'll have to plant those with more space for them to spread out, next year. Fellow who sold me the seeds didn't think to mention that."

Worse, as Arthur soon discovered, the stems were studded all over with tiny, abrasive spikes, so they had the means to defend themselves against an unwary movement among them.

So, he needed his eyes clear in order to move safely from one squash to the next, looking for the small black bodies of the beetles that Mister Hillyard had instructed him to pick off and flick into the hereafter with a forefinger and thumb.

What he didn't much need were his mental energies, and so those found employment in pondering the question of how it was that both Mister and Missus Hillyard had thought it appropriate to leave Constance alone with a suitor.

Such a thing would have been unthinkable in the community where Arthur had grown up, as it would have immediately brought the young woman's honor under suspicion. As he considered the question, though, he was reminded of a conversation he'd had with one of his squad members on the long march from Saratoga . . . and inevitably, that thought reminded him of what had come to pass later that same day.

They had been making decent time for a change, as despite threatening skies, the road was mercifully dry. Miller, one of the few members of Arthur's original squad still with him, struck up a conversation. "I think that the worst part is the gawking in the towns as we pass."

Arthur gave a harsh bark of laughter. "If a few evil eyes are the worst you've experienced, I'd say that you've been shy of the battlefields, save that I saw you there myself. Let them gawk. They've likely never seen a properly-turned out army before, nor any gentlemen of England."

"I heard a funny tale about one of our gentlemen and these colonials, now that you mention that."

"Does it involve bundling?"

"D'you mean, like wood?"

"Nay, Mister Miller, 'tis the term the colonials use for the practice of sharing a bed when they are in short supply."

Miller's eyebrows went up. "You must have been speaking to an officer, were there beds involved in the story, rather than just a pallet on the hard, cold ground."

Arthur smiled and answered, "Indeed, and if I'm honest, I'd confess that a true bed would likely just keep me awake, so accustomed am I to the comforts of a rock between the ribs and a root for a pillow. Never mind sharing a bed with a woman I've no prior acquaintance of. These New-Englanders have a strange sense of propriety, from the stories I've heard."

Miller guffawed, saying, "Oh-ho, you left out that detail. I imagine that the officer was quite happy to share that story, then."

Shaking his head, Arthur said, "Nay, he claimed that he declined and took his rest on the floor besides."

"A true gentleman, then," Miller said gravely, before his face broke into a wide grin. "More a gentleman than I should have been under that temptation."

"Well, perhaps that is why you are a private soldier, and not an officer with a commission and all that comes with it," Arthur teased, with a twinkle in his eye.

The other man shrugged. "That may be, corporal. In any event, my story is nowhere near so provocative, though I wager it may be as funny, in its own way."

Arthur gave him a wry smile, and Miller continued. "That last town where we were put up for the night, our own Lord Napier was boarded in a house at the sufferance of the owner, and a group of likely lasses appeared at the door. They said they had heard that a lord was among the guests of the house, and demanded to meet him."

Miller grinned. "You will recall that it rained all the day, and so none of us were all that neat in our appearance, having marched through the mud and downpour since the sunrise. Well, our Lord Napier was prevailed upon to make an appearance, and one of his friends presented him as though he were playing the role of a herald at arms."

Miller gave an elaborate bow as he marched, and spoke in a deep voice not his own, "'I present to you the Right Honorable Francis Lord Napier,' the which he followed with a whole catalog of the lordship's titles and some others besides, made up on the spot for the benefit of the ladies."

He chuckled and said, "The ladies were none too impressed, between the lordship's travel-worn appearance and their perception that they were being played for fools. After a moment, one of them said, 'Well, for my part, it that be a Lord, well, then, I should like never to see any other Lord but my Lord Jehovah, and none of these sorts that walk the earth and carry bits of it along with them.'"

Miller cracked into raucous laughter at his own account, and was still wheezing when one of the American soldiers approached and demanded, "What is so all-fired funny about being a prisoner of these United States?"

Miller, with the long-practiced air of a man accustomed to fast thinking in order to cover up misdeeds, adopted the innocent expression that was so familiar to Arthur in his dealings with the man. "Why, I was just having a chuckle at the antics of one of our party, a happy remembrance if you like, as he is back behind us, pushing up your flowers of the field."

The American pursed his lips, clearly suspicious that he was being made sport of, and Arthur did his best to maintain his own serious expression as he spoke up. "This is one of my men, sir, and I will see to it that his demeanor is more in keeping with our circumstance henceforth."

The American glared now at Arthur, but after a moment he nodded briskly. "See that you do. I have observed the way that all of you invaders look at us, as though you are our betters, and it doesn't sit right, given that it is we who are marching you off as our prisoners."

"I take your meaning, sir, and I mean no disrespect. Our general has signed an acknowledgment that your forces defeated us on a fair field of battle. You are our captors, and as such are owed respect and deference as befits your station in life."

Arthur held the young man's eyes for a long moment, before the American broke his gaze and motioned back to the position from where he'd come. "I've no time to match words with you, prisoner, but you are correct that we are owed respect, just as you lot are owed the honors of war. You fought well, and lost gallantly, and no more can any commander ask of his troops." He turned away abruptly, returning to his position outside of the column of British prisoners.

When the American was out of earshot, Miller leaned over and asked, "Did you mean one word of that, Corporal?"

Arthur permitted himself the smallest of smiles. "Not a single one."

They had to find their entertainment where they could, as the weather and terrain seemed determined to inflict cruelties beyond what the battlefield could on them. It was not enough that the men of the enemy forces had tried to kill them — the very countryside sought to extract its toll for the privilege of being marched over it.

It had been that same evening when Jameson's wife had given birth in the middle of a snowstorm. The memory of that afternoon and night, and of Miller's letter, gave Arthur a fresh pang of sadness and a shiver, even as he wiped away another rivulet of sweat, standing in the midst of the squash patch and dispatching another beetle.

His men had been making their way up the slope of a particularly steep hill, and the clouds overhead had abruptly darkened in menacing heaviness. Jameson had made his way to Arthur's side and remarked to him, "Looks like it could snow, corporal."

Arthur looked up at the clouds, and agreed, "They do look very much like the clouds back home just before they give us a proper icing-down."

"I should hope that it don't do that while we're still on this hill. The wagons will ne'er make it o'er the top, if it do."

Arthur glanced over his shoulder at the supply wagons, laden with not only the baggage, but with the camp followers. The horses plodded along placidly, and Arthur reassured the man, "I don't think that you need worry for your bag, Mister Jameson."

"Oh, t'aint my bag that I am worrying after, corporal. It's my wife, d'you see? She's great with child, and her pains have started. The women have her set up in a wagon and they're caring for her as they can, but I should be very grateful to the heavens if they could but give us time to set up camp for the night 'fore the storm hits."

Arthur's eyebrows went up. "Wife, you say? How did I fail to know this about you, Mister Jameson?"

The man grinned. "Can't have you knowing everything about me, corporal, now, can I? In any event, she's just a little thing, so she don't take up much space nor eat much food. Hardly worth mentioning to you, when you've so much else on your mind." His expression turning more somber, he added, "So perhaps you could put in a good word with Himself on my behalf?" He pointed up to the sullen grey clouds.

Arthur hardly felt that he had any greater access to God than Jameson had, but he nodded anyway. "I shall do so, of course, and add to your own prayers." It did no harm to indulge the man, and he saw Jameson's relief in the way his shoulders relaxed.

"Thankee, Corporal." He withdrew to a rank closer to the carts, moving swiftly enough that the American guard never even noticed that he was out of place.

Despite the best efforts given by both Jameson and Arthur in bargaining with the heavens for a little more time to travel on passable roads, it was not a quarter-hour later that the first fat, wet flakes of snow were falling heavily onto Arthur's nose. Within minutes, he could scarcely see the trees on the far side of the road, so heavy was the snowfall.

Not long after that, he heard shouting and commotion behind him, and he turned to see that a horse had lost its footing, falling and scattering the contents of the packs strapped across its back all over the road. Behind the flailing horse, he saw a wagon tip as a wheel lost the road, and another burst of profanity reached his ears.

He joined with the others helping to put things right, gathering up blankets and bags from the churned-up mud of the road, and adding his shoulder to those helping to push the cart back onto the roadway. The whole column of men and the baggage train alike had stopped as a result of the disruption. When the Americans ordered them into motion again, several of the carts were mired in the mud, and it took more hard shoulder work to get them moving again.

The pattern repeated several times through the afternoon, until finally, the Americans relented and called a halt, seeming to begrudge the necessity when there were still hours of daylight remaining.

Looking over the chaos of the men slogging through snow now rising well up the sides of their boots, Arthur spotted Jameson wringing his hands beside a wagon, an officer standing beside him, looking concerned, but unsure how he might help.

Approaching the pair, Arthur heard the keening wail of a woman's voice, and he picked up his pace, sliding and skidding through the snow. He put his hand on Jameson's shoulder, and the man whirled around, panic in his eyes.

"She can't wait any longer for us to get to a proper house where she can be delivered of the babe," Jameson insisted. "She's a-going to have it right here on the road, and with this weather, too!"

Arthur glanced around the side of the open-topped wagon, and saw a slight woman, her belly distended with the child who was so eager to enter the world. She was clutching the hands of two women on either side of her, as as flakes of snow fell through the branches of the trees that were already bent with its weight, Arthur could see that something had to be done.

He turned to Jameson. "Can you get at some oilcloth from one of the other wagons? We'll need a sheet of it large enough to rig over this wagon for your wife."

Some of the wild fear faded from Jameson's eyes as he took on the look of a man with a purpose. "Oh, aye, that I can. Give me but a minute."

Turning to the officer next, Arthur said, "Sir, could you help me secure some ropes to the sides of the wagon, so that we can pull them across the top and thus secure the cloth?"

The officer—an aristocratic-looking fellow with a lieutenant's insignia on his epaulettes and bearing an expression of shocked curiosity as he stared at the scene within the wagon — started ever so slightly, as though he had not even been aware of Arthur's presence.

"Huh? What's that? Oh, yes, certainly."

"Thank you, sir." Arthur reached past the officer to retrieve a rope coiled in the bed of the wagon and handed it to the man, loosening the free end. He secured it tightly to the upright post at one corner of the back of the wagon, and then took the remaining rope from the lieutenant's hands.

"Hold this fast, sir, as I secure it over the other side." He grabbed the knot to indicate where he wanted the officer to put his hands, and then moved over to the other side of the wagon, glancing inside as the laboring woman gave another agonized wail.

He shook his head to keep himself focused on the task at hand and busied himself with the rope, winding it about the opposite back post on the wagon.

By the time Jameson had returned with a wadded-up oilcloth clutched to his chest, Arthur was satisfied with the ropes that crisscrossed tautly over the open space above the bed of the wagon and the women in it.

He took the oilcloth from Jameson and unfolded it, pleased to see that it was actually a little larger than he needed. He then caught the officer's gaze. "Sir, if you can take the other side, while Mister Jameson holds the back, we can lift this over the top, and then secure it with the remaining rope."

The lieutenant wordlessly took the corner of the cloth from him, still seeming to be in shock at the sight of a woman laboring under these conditions.

Together, the three men enclosed the top of the wagon with the oilcloth, providing the women with at least some rudimentary shelter from the storm.

"We'll be needing some light now, sir, and thank you very kindly," one of the women called out, and Arthur almost thought she sounded peevish that the same oilcloth that sheltered her from the storm — intensifying again as a band of thicker snow passed over the camp — had cut off what light the waning afternoon offered.

Keeping his own irritation out of his voice, he called back, "Right away, of course."

He turned to Jameson, sensing that it was a blessing to distract him from the pained cries his wife was more regularly emitting. "Find a signal lamp and mind that you get its owner to light it for you before you accept it. Two would be even better."

The lieutenant spoke up. "Find Sergeant Guiles, and tell him that Anburey said to give you the lamps."

"Aye, sir," Jameson said, and again hurried off.

The lieutenant seemed to have recovered himself, and was slowly shaking his head as he turned to Arthur. "You seem to have matters in hand, dire though they seemed when first I came upon this scene."

Arthur answered briskly, "I am only doing my duty to a fellow soldier of the army, sir. The need was obvious, and the means were readily at hand."

He gave the other man a quick, sardonic smile. "Our lot is accustomed to thinking in terms of tents and the like for shelter. Had there been a house nearby, I assure you that we would have been bound for that instead, but this will answer adequately for this evening."

Jameson was back already with two tin lamps, light shining through the gaps around the door, and through the multitude of holes punched through the sides. "Guiles made me swear to return them come morning, but he even gave me an extra candle for each one when I told him what I needed them for."

Arthur nodded, smiling at the man. "Give them to the women inside, then, and let us see whether we can find something warm to drink, all right?" Turning to the lieutenant, he asked, "Should you like to join us, sir?"

"Oh, no, I couldn't possibly," the officer said, "I need to return to my captain, as he is doubtless already convinced that I have contrived to fall off the mountainside."

He turned to leave, and then whirled around suddenly. "Please inform me when she has given birth, and relieve my concern for both her and the babe."

Arthur touched his knuckle to his forehead respectfully. "I will gladly do so, sir, and thank you for your assistance, both with rigging the shelter, and with securing the lamps." The lieutenant acknowledged the salute with a slight bow, and walked away, disappearing into the swirling snow.

Arthur put his hand on Jameson's shoulder. The prospective father was again peering into the back of the wagon, that expression of panic overtaking his face once more. "Come. Worrying yourself to death will not change the events of the night. The squad should have our tents raised, and I'm pretty sure I can get some rum from Missus Kelly, both to stave off the cold and to steady your nerves."

Jameson gave him a grateful, if nervous, smile, and with one last glance into the back of the wagon, followed the corporal back to where their squad was encamped.

Arthur flicked another beetle away angrily at the memory, and wondered idly what Lieutenant Anburey would have to say if he learned that Jameson's own commander had barred the soldier's wife and son from getting medical attention and fated them to share in a common grave.

Who was the inhuman actor in that tragedy, and who was the one who'd held out the possibility of salvation? Keeping the villains straight from the heroes in his mind was sometimes a difficult practice.

The Americans may have fallen short in their obligations to care for their prisoner, but had show human kindness in their offer to secure care for his family. The British officer had been utterly correct in his demand for medical attention to his soldier, but had sacrificed an innocent woman and her son in order to make a point.

It might all have been in vain anyway, though, as camp fevers rarely relented even in the face of competent physicking. Still, propriety should have been observed by giving as much care as possible to all three who were lost.

Arthur sighed and stooped to send another beetle to its oblivion. At least in the battle against pests, the lines were clear.

Chapter 13

That night over dinner at the kitchen table, Mister Hillyard was in a downright jovial mood, though he made a show of tamping down his exuberance as he related the cause for his happiness.

"Heard from Mister Gibbs that Contant was complaining about my having thrashed his son."

"Oh?" Missus Hillyard paused in dishing out the boiled pudding to look up sharply at her husband, and Constance looked away, appearing to Arthur as though she were suddenly nauseous.

"Aye, said that I broke the boy's nose, and that the younger Contant could not be expected to explain what might have driven me to assault him until it has healed. However, he claimed that there was no possible cause for me to have given such treatment to his poor, innocent son." Mister Hillyard emphasized this last by drawing out the words into a near-whine, and then rolled his eyes.

"I hope that you disabused Mister Gibbs of the notion that you are taken to fits of violence without cause?"

"Oh, yes, of course. I gave Gibbs a full accounting of the boy's transgressions. By the end of our conversation, I think that he was ready to ride out for the Contant place and add to Jack's injuries, but I told him that I was well-satisfied that he would not be likely to again think he could take such advantage of a girl."

Constance spoke up then, her voice uncharacteristically

wan and bleak. "I shouldn't be so certain, Papa. He spoke to me as though I were a thing owed to him, and when I spurned his advances, he took what he wanted without evincing the slightest sliver of guilt."

Mister Hillyard's face was suddenly grey, and Arthur felt certain that it reflected the same bloodless sensation that had washed over him at Constance's plain words.

She continued, her tone still quiet and matter-of-fact, "When I screamed and he realized that the noise had raised you from your bed, that was when he struck me. It did not seem to have been an expression of regret for his actions, but rather taking out on me his anger at having been thwarted in continuing them at his leisure."

She shook her head, her gaze fixed on something visible only to her, out beyond the window. "No, I do not believe that the thrashing you delivered to him, no matter how well-deserved, will make him more likely to treat any more gently the next girl with whom he has an opportunity to have his way — though it may make him more wary about the circumstances under which he tries her."

His jaw clenched, Mister Hillyard grated out, "Then I shall have to ensure that he does not have such an opportunity with any other girl."

Missus Hillyard spoke up then, her tone sharp. "And how do you propose to do that, Mister Hillyard? While the Council of Safety may take little notice of a boy who oversteps the bounds of decency with a girl, they will not so lightly overlook a murder."

The muscles in Mister Hillyard's jaw jumped, but he did not reply immediately.

Arthur made bold enough to speak up. "A man need not

die to be rendered incapable of assaulting a woman. There were plenty of jokes passed around camp of the risks of having something precious carried off by an unlucky shot from the other side, yet those gibes had a foundation of truth behind them." He smiled grimly. "But I suppose that your Council of Safety would look no more favorably on such a wound being inflicted."

"Nay, nor would it stop the boy from visiting some other nature of violence on another woman," Constance reasoned. "I believe truly that what — what he did to me was not simply a matter of satisfying his bestial urges, but was a means of imposing his will upon me. When it became clear that his little flatteries were not going to persuade me to give willingly what he was after, he hesitated not a moment to take it instead." She flushed deep red at the memory, and her eyes were bright with unshed tears.

Missus Hillyard reached across the table to squeeze her daughter's hand. "There can be no apology sufficient for what you have suffered, my dear Constance, but your Papa and I will carry to our graves the sorrow of having exposed you to such a hazard."

Constance shook her head emphatically. "Don't, Mama. It was not you or Papa who authored the attack on me. The responsibility lies with Mister Contant alone, and he will answer to a higher justice in due time. Between now and that happy day, though, I only wish that there were something we could do that would save another woman from his vile clutches."

Mister Hillyard sighed. "The best we can likely hope for is to prevent him from hurting anyone who might hear our warnings of his monstrous conduct."

Missis Hillyard frowned and answered, "All that is likely to accomplish is to ensure that he hurts some poor girl beyond the reach of our words. Still, it is better than doing nothing at all."

Her husband grimaced, but said nothing, and after that, it was as if by an unspoken agreement that they all let the subject drop.

A rumble of thunder rolled across the fields outside, offering an opportunity for a welcome change of topic. "I hope that the storm doesn't sour the milk from goats like my Ma always said it did the cows back home," Arthur said, with a faint smile of remembrance.

"Not that I've ever noticed," Missus Hillyard said.

"Your people back in Britain kept cows, did they?" Mister Hillyard seemed as eager as Arthur for conversation on safer ground.

"Oh, aye," Arthur nodded. My Da is a smallholder there, with a farm not unlike yours, only more wind and less sun. Your farm is larger, but we still make space for one milch cow. She never liked storms, though, and Ma always told us not to drink of her milk after there had been a great boomer."

Constance spoke up suddenly. "Do you miss it terribly?"

Arthur shrugged. "When I joined up, it was because I knew I would never inherit the farm, unless some awful fate befell both of my brothers. I knew, too, that I might never return home, but for a short visit, subject to the needs of the service. I was not eager to make that sacrifice, but it was the best option my circumstances offered."

He sighed and squinted thoughtfully. "I miss the great vistas of one hill after another of well-tended land, each square inch devoted to some purposeful use by men who lived before my grandfather was born. There's a somber grandeur to it, one that's missing in this new, untamed land."

He glanced over at Mister Hillyard, adding hastily, "No offense intended, naturally, sir."

Mister Hillyard raised a hand, waving off the apology. "None taken, Mister Leary. I should be very much surprised if our countries were so similar as to be indistinguishable."

Arthur let pass unchallenged the implicit suggestion that England and New-England now represented entirely different countries, but only added, "'Tis passing strange to be in a place where nearly every building is so new that one can practically smell the sawdust, when I came up accustomed to houses having heritages of hundreds of years, and generations of families."

Mister Hillyard smiled gently. "Aye, I suppose so, and yet, there is something appealing about a place where a man can make his own mark, rather than being constrained by the press of history."

Arthur nodded. "I reckon I can understand that well enough. Not far from my village, there are the tumbled-down old walls that the Romans built to keep themselves safe from the Scots, who, it is said, were even less civilized in those times than they are in these. The old wall stretches out from one shore of England clear across to the other, and there are many who still regard it as a wound upon the land, and who do what they can to undo its control over our movements."

He shrugged. "As for my family, my grandfather valued it for the regularity of its blocks, which he found of great utility when he needed to build a new barn. Those old Romans knew a thing or two about building straight and level."

Mister Hillyard smiled. "I suppose they must have, for

their works to have survived to the present day, some dozens of centuries later."

"Perhaps only one dozen centuries, give or take, if I remember my lessons aright," Arthur replied. "Still, those Roman ways were an imposition on the people in that place. It's no wonder that they were eventually sent packing."

He paused, realizing that he was starting to give his host a compelling argument against his own cause, and smiled ruefully to himself.

Although Mister Hillyard did not give any sign of having found a greater significance in his words, Constance caught his eye and gave him a playful, quick smile.

"*Sic semper tyrannis*, hmm?"

Arthur ducked his head and flushed. "I never did learn any of the Latin, I'm afraid, Miss Hillyard. My schooling was concluded before I could get very far past *agricola, agricolae*, for it seemed unlikely that I'd ever be more than a farmer myself."

She smiled fully at him now. "There is no shame in being a farmer, and indeed 'tis farming that gave Papa the means to ensure that I did get some Latin."

Arthur enjoyed the way her smile lit up her face, though her comment reminded him of a conversation he'd had with one of the jägers as they'd taken their ease following a long day on the road from Saratoga. The man had been full of wonder at the wealth of even the common man in New-England.

"Have you seen of their tables? The poorest farmer even, he breakfasts on roasted meat, fresh milk from the morning, apples baked in the coals, and plate after plate of butter cakes. In Hesse, a nobleman is eating so good hardly!" The man's cheeks were red from the cold air, and he was huddled within his clothes, but even half-hidden, Arthur could see the amazement in the German's eyes.

He offered, "Perhaps they put on a feast to for a show to impress upon you how well they eat?"

"No, we asked, and the farmers all say no, they eat this way every day, need full bellies for to do the work of the farm." The jäger frowned and added, "When little I was, a full day's work I did whether my belly was full or not."

Arthur's own childhood had been much the same, and he had observed nothing in his time in America that had contradicted the jäger's observation.

The Hillyard farm was remarkable only to his eyes — in comparison to the Contant farm, Mister Hillyard seemed to think it was only modestly successful.

He nodded back to Constance. "I've seen for myself how rich the soil and wildlife are here. As grand as the vistas are back home, they do not harbor such natural gifts."

Mister Hillyard spoke up now. "A man who is willing to work hard can quite readily make a prosperous life for himself here." He seemed to pick his next words carefully. "My young friend, do not take my words awry, but there is opportunity here in America for a young man such as yourself. None will long remember how you came to be here, should you decide to stay and prove out your own grant in time."

Arthur said nothing, only pursing his lips in thought.

Mister Hillyard wasn't wrong — the potential of starting fresh, setting aside the difficult and dangerous work of being a soldier, and trying to find some means by which he could secure a small holding for himself here had more than once crossed his mind. However, abandoning his duty, and committing the very act of desertion which he'd once warned the men of his squad was death to undertake was a disquieting thought.

Before he could give voice to any of these considerations, though, Mister Hillyard added, "For my part, I'd be happy to have you as a neighbor, should it come to that." He stood, slapping his hands on the table. "And with that thought, I will retire to my bed for the night, so that I can return to the work of making the most of these opportunities when the sun rises tomorrow."

Arthur rose with the others, and mumbled his good nights on his way out to a long night of staring into the darkness from his pallet, with only the grey cat for company, as he wondered what the future might hold.

Chapter 14

The next afternoon, Arthur was drawing a sledge laden with goat droppings over the field, shoveling them out in as even a distribution as he could manage. He was grateful that they did not have the reek of fresh cow manure, and Mister Hillyard assured him that the small pellets of waste wouldn't hurt the next crop going in, despite being fresh.

Back home, Arthur knew, manure from the cows must be permitted to age for a year and more before it was safe to use on the fields.

Arthur looked up when he'd reached the spot where he'd left off with the last load, and grunted to himself in surprise. A squat, solidly-built man, whose greying curls were cropped tightly to his head under a hat nearly as dandy as Jack Contant's had been had appeared on the road.

The stranger's rapid, purposeful gait and grim expression instantly suggested to Arthur's eye that he brought trouble. The man spotted Arthur almost at the same time, and stomped his way to the stone fence nearest where he was working.

He called out, his voice harsh and unpleasant, "You there — is your master about? I've business with him that will not wait."

Arthur had learned in his time in the army that what was a crisis for another man need not represent a matter of urgency for himself. So he took his time, loading up and carefully broadcasting a shovel full of manure across the field, and then setting the shovel down deliberately on the sledge before wiping his hands down his breeches and approaching the fence.

"What was it that you needed of me, sir?"

"Are you daft, boy? I asked whether your master is about. I require his attention to an urgent matter of honor."

Arthur let his eyebrows rise. "Honor, sir? Do you mean to challenge my master to a duel, or is there perhaps a more delicate term I ought use when I inform him of your request?"

He thought to himself that the man should probably not indulge his temper so much, as it looked as though the veins on the sides of his face might burst. After staring Arthur down for a long moment, the visitor finally snapped, "Just tell him that Mister Contant is here to see about my son."

Arthur could feel his own brows disappear under his cap. "Contant, you say? And you speak of honor? A curious thing to hear, indeed. You may wait here, while I go and see if my master can free himself from his current tasks in order to make time to come and speak with you of *honor.*"

With that, Arthur coldly spun on his heel and strode across the field toward the barn, where he knew Mister Hillyard was looking after the cow. He did not trust himself to remain in the other man's presence for another moment, lest he say something that really might lead to a duel — no matter that such contests were strictly illegal in New-England.

In the dim light of the barn, he could see that the cow's stall stood open, and he approached. "Mister Hillyard?"

The farmer appeared at the entry to the pen, answering, "Yes, Mister Leary?"

Arthur spoke carefully. "Mister Contant is waiting by the fence around the field, and wants to speak to you about his son. He claims that it is urgent, and even said it was a matter of honor."

Mister Hillyard fairly sprang out of the stall, growling, "Why, I'll show him honor, that rotten rat of a man." Arthur could see him casting about with his eyes for something he could use as a weapon, before he asked sharply, "Was he armed?"

"Not that I could see, no."

"Worse luck. I shall be obliged to meet him similarly unarmed, but if he so much as utters one word about his so-called *honor*, I may just thrash him with my hands, as I did his son."

"I shouldn't be surprised if you did, Mister Hillyard. Shall I see to the cow?"

Mister Hillyard retrieved a cloth from the stall door and carefully wiped off his hands with it. "Please do, and then return to the field, that you might at least discourage Mister Contant from any thoughts of doing further violence to our family by your presence." He chuckled. "You might also restrain me from doing any further violence to his."

"Aye, sir."

Mister Hillyard stomped out of the barn, and Arthur glanced into the cow's stall. It appeared that the farmer had been checking her over, as she was due to calf any day now. Arthur approached her, speaking quiet nonsense so that she wouldn't take surprise at his appearance, and patted her side as he approached her head.

She was much more interested in the grain that Mister Hillyard had put down for her than in anything that Arthur was doing, so he quickly untied her and coiled up the rope around his arm, leaving her to finish her treat.

He closed the door to the stall, ensuring that the latch was secure, and hung the rope on a peg beside the door before following Mister Hillyard out into the light of day outside.

He saw the farmer standing a distance away from Mister Contant, and he could already hear the other man's shouts. He couldn't quite make out what he was saying, though, so he approached more closely, feigning his return to the sledge. From there, he could hear every word of Contant's accusations.

"Jack went out hunting yesterday morning, and I expected him back by nightfall, with a brace of pheasant for our supper. Instead, Missus Contant and I have neither seen nor heard anything from him since the moment he closed the door, and I knew at once that you must have done something to him."

"Me, sir? I have had the satisfaction of breaking your son's face for his vile assault upon my daughter, but I have no designs on pursuing any further justice against him, so long as he keeps his distance and never again steps foot on my property."

"So you say, Mister Hillyard, but I've only your word on any of these matters. All I know is that Jack told us the next morning that you would no longer entertain his suit for marriage. Then you showed up and thrashed him — a grown man, beating another man's son! — and I had to call out the barber to physic his nose."

"We had a fine understanding, you and I, until you decided that your little strumpet of a daughter was too good for my boy, and —"

Whatever Contant was going to add was cut off, as Mister Hillyard closed the distance between them with two fast strides and swung at the other man.

Contant stumbled and fell onto his backside, his hat flying into the dirt behind him. He may have eluded Mister Hillyard's fist, but not his words.

"You will never again mention my daughter, if you don't want to be thrown out for the pigs to dine upon, sir. What your son did to her was beyond the pale of civilized behavior, and I am only shocked to discover that I failed to perceive that he was raised by a man as crude and unrefined as he himself has become."

Contant scrambled to his feet, and Arthur recognized the swollen vein that popped at the side of the man's forehead before he answered, his voice a hoarse scream. "You dare threaten me, and to heap abuse upon me, after whatever you did to my son? Do you say you would feed me to your pigs, sir? Should we look to your pigsty for my boy's wretched remains?"

Mister Hillyard laughed aloud at his neighbor. "Mister Contant, you ought know that I do not even have any swine, much less would I actually feed you to them if I did. No, sir, I give my animals only wholesome foodstuff, and would never risk the health of an honest sow by offering her such a meal."

Mister Hillyard shook his head, still chuckling while Mister Contant struggled to find the words to answer this insult.

The farmer did not give the other man a chance to reply, though, saying, "I've done nothing to your boy, haven't even seen him since I bruised my knuckles upon his face. In truth, I haven't stirred from my farm in days, as I find plenty to occupy me here."

He motioned to Arthur, beckoning him to approach.

Arthur put down the shovel again, having used it for precisely nothing except as an excuse to eavesdrop, and joined

Mister Hillyard.

"Mister Leary, I don't suppose that the boy who despoiled my innocent daughter has made a return to this farm, and you failed to mention it to me?"

"Nay, Mister Hillyard." Arthur didn't add that if Jack Contant *had* returned to the property, he wouldn't have bothered to feed his remains to pigs, even if there had been some on the farm. There was no lack of places where a deep grave would be easy enough to dig, after all, and he'd had plenty of experience in efficiently burying bodies in the aftermath of Saratoga.

It didn't seem like a good idea to mention that under the circumstances, though.

Mister Hillyard turned back to Contant. "See? Nobody's seen him, and none of us have left the farm in the time since your boy went out. It seems more likely that he wandered into trouble of some sort, and is nursing a freshly rebroken nose or a blacked eye, too ashamed to come home even to a father like you."

Contant sputtered, "You forget yourself, sir!"

Mister Hillyard just smiled grimly. "Nay, sir, you forget yourself. You are the one who raised a boy instead of a man, and failed to properly teach him to treat a woman with suitable regard. You are the one who set loose upon the world a son who thinks it acceptable to take what he pleases, and to strike a woman when she rebuffs him. And you are the one who believed the lies that boy told about his actions, and who failed to mete out the appropriate justice to him."

Mister Hillyard fixed Contant with a glare. "Why, sir, if I had a son who had done what your boy did, I would have been at the door of the girl's father with my hat in hand, begging to know how I could start to make up for the crimes that my blood had inflicted on the world."

He pointed to the road, his finger forming a line from his shoulder as straight and firm as the line of his mouth. "Get off my land, and don't you ever think to make accusations against me or my family again. You have done enough already, sir, and I will be well-satisfied if I never clap eyes upon you again in this life."

Contant seemed to consider making some answer, but thought better of it, turned, and retrieved his hat from the dirt before he hurried away down the road and out of sight.

After the man had disappeared, Mister Hillyard finally dropped his outstretched arm, and Arthur was surprised to see a tremor in the farmer's hand as he relaxed. "Mister Leary, it is at a moment like this when I wish I were the type of person who kept whiskey or rum in supply in my home. I could surely use a healthy tot of either after that interview."

Arthur said nothing — he did not think that Mister Hillyard expected him to reply — but followed the farmer into the house as directed by a motion of the man's still-shaking hand.

Inside, Mister Hillyard made for Constance's jug of switchel and lifted it directly to his mouth, not even bothering with a cup. When he had drunk his fill, he lowered the jug, wiped his mouth, and offered the jug over. Arthur accepted it gratefully.

Though it was but refreshing and not intoxicating, he found it most welcome. An ale or even a tot of rum would have been more welcome, but this was no mean substitute.

Missus Hillyard and Constance had stopped chopping vegetables for supper to stare at the men openly. Missus Hillyard seemed about to say something, but her husband raised a hand to forestall her objections.

"We had a visitor," he said, by way of explanation, adding, "Our neighbor, Mister Contant."

Constance gasped, and her father reached out to pat her shoulder reassuringly.

"The father, not the son. It appears that the boy has gone missing, and his father's suspicion fell immediately upon me, by reason of my having been the most recent person to have thrashed him."

He smiled grimly. "I disabused Mister Contant of his notion that I'd had anything to do with his boy's absence, and indeed, I told him that I thought it likely that his son was hiding away after having gotten another beating for some fresh crime."

Missus Hillyard asked, "Do you really think that's likely?"

Her husband shrugged. "It's as likely as anything else. It's also possible that the boy drowned and was swept away in a river, that he followed some girl into Boston, or even that he took it into his head to join the militia — though that last would require a sense of duty that I doubt he could ever muster of himself."

"Nay, never," Arthur found himself saying. "No militia unit worthy of the name would accept a man of so little substance as Jack Contant."

He grimaced. "I saw enough of your militias to have developed a respect for their discipline, at least, and that would seem to be Mister Contant's least evident quality."

Mister Hillyard nodded in agreement. "You make a fine point. In any event, it is neither our concern nor in our interest to inquire very deeply as to what has become of Jack. If someone has sent him into the hereafter — which is another quite plausible possibility — we should not like to look as though we approve."

Missus Hillyard said sharply, "I should very much approve, and I don't care who knows it."

Mister Hillyard gave her a sympathetic look, but said firmly, "We must care who knows that we wish Mister Contant ill, because if some ill fortune has befallen him, it would do none of us any good to be under suspicion of having had a hand in it."

He smiled faintly and gave a tiny shake of his head. "I doubt that he has met the fate that he so richly deserves, though. It is by far most likely that he is sleeping off a jug of rum in some strange bed, and will stumble home before supper."

He looked around the kitchen appraisingly. "Speaking of supper, we are interrupting you in the preparation of ours, and we've both still got plenty of work to do. Come, Mister Leary, enough of our gossiping. There will be time enough for speculation and wishful thinking at the table that will await us after the day's work is done."

Arthur said nothing, but only followed Mister Hillyard back outside. When the door had closed behind them, he asked, quietly, "Do you think some suspicion might fall upon us, should Mister Contant not return as you've foretold?"

Mister Hillyard squinted into the sun for a long moment as he walked, and then answered. "Oh, aye, and it wouldn't be unjustified. After all, I did break the boy's face in fisticuffs, and gave you leave to do to him as you pleased, if he returned to the scene of his crimes. What's more, I have told plenty of my friends around here what transpired, and it's wholly possible that one of them came upon Contant and did something to right the wrong."

He shrugged. "Most likely of all, though, is that we will hear from his father tomorrow — though it had best be through an intermediary, if Contant knows what's good for him — that the boy came crawling home reeking of drink and misdeeds."

Chapter 15

The morrow came, but did not bring with it any news of Jack Contant's return. Arthur worked his way around the field, hoeing in the goat manure to prepare it for planting. As usual with dull, repetitive work, the job gave him plenty of time for thought.

Although there was no end of work on the farm, there was ample food to eat, which was a thing that Arthur had learned to never again take for granted. He went to sleep each night well worn-out, but was never plagued with the hunger pangs that had been his constant companion after Saratoga.

Looking at his arms as he worked the hoe through the rich soil, he thought that he'd already filled out to something resembling his former health. Beyond simply being able to feed his family adequately from the bounty of his own land, though, it was clear that Mister Hillyard was able to trade enough — even in the midst of the convulsions of a rebellion — to maintain a comfortable lifestyle.

The things that Arthur had thought might be the marks of poverty were, he realized, simple frugality. After all, he guessed that dinner tasted as good from a tin plate as it did from fine Delftware — though he could not testify to it from personal experience — and he doubted that a crystal glass would be a better way to enjoy cold switchel than was the tin cup that was daily handed to him by a smiling friend.

As though summoned by the thought, Constance emerged from the kitchen with two cups in her hands, smiling as the breeze caught a strand of hair that had escaped from her cap and blew it across her nose. Arthur paused, leaning against the handle of the hoe and smiled in reply as she approached. In a moment, he gratefully accepted the cup that she offered to him, and took a gulp.

"Papa is going into town to buy a few things that Mama needs for the kitchen, though I think they both are just looking for excuses to see what word there may be of Mister Contant."

Arthur lowered his cup to find Constance looking at him with an anxious expression on her face. "Oh?"

"I don't know whether I'd be better satisfied should he have come to an end of some sort, or if he is sitting smugly at home, lifting any shadow of suspicion from Papa," she admitted.

Arthur placed a reassuring hand on her arm. "Whatever has become of Mister Contant, it is entirely outside of our control. There is naught to be gained by worrying on it now, and furthermore, he made the choices that placed him in whatever peril he may have faced."

Constance's face screwed up in an angry frown. "It is always *his* choices, *his* decisions, *his* actions, and I am expected to but sit passively by and wait for *his* consequences."

The anger passed from her face, and she favored Arthur with a crooked smile. "In truth, I agree with my mother, and wish Mister Contant nothing but ill. But more than that, I find I also wish that I had the opportunity to be the author of his ill fate. I should like to be the one making the decisions for once."

Arthur nodded slowly. "I can understand that, though I

should like to offer a counterpoint, if I may."

"Say on," Constance said, hiding her expression behind her cup, but Arthur could see wariness in her eyes.

"I have had the opportunity to, as you put it, be the author of the ill fate of another man." He raised a finger. "Now, before you take offense, let me point out that I was doing my duty as I understood it, and that this man was earnestly doing his duty in turn. By which I mean to say that he had a musket leveled at me, and I at him."

Constance frowned into her cup, and Arthur could see her brow furrow above it, but she said nothing, so he continued. "We came upon each other in the smoke, and we were close enough that I could hear him curse as he pulled his trigger and his gun failed to fire. Mine did not fail to fire, and he fell."

Arthur shrugged. "It is the only time that I am certain that I killed a man, though I certainly fired enough shots while both sides were yet in formations. This time, though, I heard his voice, saw him try to kill me, and beat him to the act."

He looked Constance in the eye, and found anger there, but also understanding. "Constance, the only reason that I mention this moment of my history is to tell you that this soldier has haunted me ever since, and when I think of him, I feel a sense of responsibility to be worthy to be the survivor of our encounter."

He sighed. "Make no mistake, had the spark in his pan reached the charge behind his ball, you would never have known me, other than perhaps as an anonymous grave, had you ever chanced to visit Saratoga. I am glad that I lived, and that I have come to know you and your family, but I am not glad that he died."

He lifted his gaze to the sky in contemplation. "I will

permit myself to dream of what might have been, had this war not been joined, and had I simply come to be your father's hired man through a peaceful sequence of events, and had neither that soldier nor I have been forced to stain our souls with the murder of another man."

He smiled gently, turning back to look at Constance now. "So do not wish that fortune should deliver to you the obligation or opportunity to bring about the death of another person, no matter the circumstance. Mister Contant, if he still lives, will find his own fate, and even if that is not as satisfying as it might be to help him along to it, it leaves your soul untarnished by the violence we both wish upon him."

Constance sighed. "I fear that you are a bad influence on me, Mister Leary. There was a time when I would have spat in your face at the revelation that you took the life of one of our men. Indeed, I grieve to hear it, and I will confess that my grief is entirely for the man you killed. That you suffer anguish for your act is just as unsatisfying a justice as whatever mere loss of reputation Mister Contant has suffered as Papa tells any who will listen what he has done."

She pursed her lips and drew a deep, unhappy breath. "There are no truly good men, I am learning. Each of us carries some kernel of evil in our hearts, whether we have acted upon it or are frustrated in our wish to do so."

"To the contrary, Miss Hillyard, I believe that there are very few truly evil men, and that restraint and good judgment are more common than malevolence and error. Your father did not impose the full measure of justice that I am certain his heart wished for against Mister Contant. You have not, in fact, acted to bring

Mister Contant low, despite your wish to do so . . . and I did not fire indiscriminately at all who I saw on the field of battle, but only upon orders and on the most dire and immediate of threat."

"What of Mister Contant? Will you now try to convince me that he acted with any restraint or good judgment?"

"Not much, I will confess. But another, worse man might have done you far more grave harm than even he did. You have the chance to build a life not defined by the actions of another. Not all get that chance."

Constance frowned thoughtfully for a long time, and finally sighed deeply. "I never thought that I would take lessons in how to be a better person from a soldier sent to put down our revolution against the Crown, but these are strange times."

She looked down into her cup and tossed back the last of her switchel. "In any event, is there anything that I should ask Papa to fetch back from town that you might need for your work?"

Arthur shook his head. "I've all that your father has seen fit to provide me with, and if there is something I'll need in order to get done what needs doing, I am confident he's aware of it already and will trade accordingly."

"Aye, but 'tis polite to ask."

He bowed his head in a gesture of thanks. "I am far more eager for what news he might bring back."

She gathered up his empty cup and turned to leave, saying over her shoulder, "As are we all."

When Mister Hillyard walked back from the road up to the house on his return from town, he bore a troubled expression, and Arthur didn't even pretend to have some innocent reason to follow him to the door. Mister Hillyard nodded to him, motioning him to come in and join the family at the table.

Missus Hillyard and Constance were already working on dinner, but they set that work aside to sit and hear what the head of the household had to report.

The farmer drew a deep breath, and then said, "Well, he hasn't turned up." Missus Hillyard and Constance exchanged a worried glance as Mister Hillyard continued. "But someone did find his gun and his hat, out in the woods, and there were signs of an almighty struggle nearby."

He hesitated, and then plunged on, saying in a rush, "There was a not inconsiderable amount of blood on the ground there. They found no body, but I think it is safe to presume that we will never again see Jack Contant in this life."

Missus Hillyard's face bore a stunned look, and Constance, unaccountably burst into tears. Mister Hillyard rose and pulled her into an embrace, his face a rictus of pain for his daughter's anguish. Missus Hillyard joined him, enfolding their daughter in comfort and support.

For his part, Arthur couldn't quite be certain what he was feeling. Not sorrow, certainly, nor any particular satisfaction. There was a small part of him that was glad at the thought that Contant would never hurt another woman as he'd hurt Constance, but he also had the thought that whatever had happened to the man, it still wasn't a full measure of justice for his acts.

Mostly, though, he realized that what he was feeling was relief. The wild thing that had splashed Contant's blood about — Arthur's squad had been warned to be on the lookout for bears and cougars — had saved those around this table from needing to do anything. Even if it had been a man, perhaps a friend of Mister

Hillyard's spurred into action by the account of Constance's ordeal, the stain he had spoken to her of was not borne by her or her father.

Whatever had happened to Contant, it had lifted whatever obligation either Mister Hillyard or Arthur himself might have felt to take further action against the man for his future acts.

More importantly, his future acts would never include any further harm to Miss Hillyard. She could put him and his violations of her person firmly into her past.

Despite what Arthur had said to her, he understood that what she had gone through would likely mark her for life, in one way or another, but at the very least, it was now definitively over and done with.

Chapter 16

No new information came to light regarding Jack Contant's fate, and absent a corpse, his father couldn't even have a proper funeral. If they hadn't been such awful men, Arthur might have felt bad for them. He did spare a prayer for Missus Contant, though, who not only had to endure her husband's boorishness, but had lost her son, now, too.

In the meantime, the ebb and flow of life on the Hillyard farm continued unabated.

If Arthur had found mowing arduous, and raking had seemed like divine punishment, the work of threshing was endless, mindless torment. It was true that he'd taken part in threshing bees back at home, but here on the farm, it was just Mister Hillyard, himself, and Constance. She had insisted on doing her part, taking a turn with the unceasing motion of the flail against the stalks of barley on the barn floor.

Mowing it a few days after Contant's disappearance had, at least gone smoothly. Arthur felt quite at home with the scythe in his hand now, and could lay down an even swathe of the grain the first time through. When it was cut, he'd expected with trepidation that Mister Hillyard would then give him the rake again.

After he'd put the scythe away, though, the farmer had emerged empty-handed from the barn.

At Arthur's confused expression, the man had smiled and

asked, "You've not harvested barley before, then?"

"Nay, I've not. The closest I've come is threshing the wheat that my father had his men actually cut."

"Well," the farmer grinned, "you've got the opportunity to learn something new today, then. Watch and learn."

Starting at the first swathe, he bent and gathered up a double handful of the barley stalks, straightening and compressing them until he could readily hold them tightly in one big hand. He plucked out a few stalks and twisted them together to form a makeshift cord, and wrapped it around the cluster of stalks in his hand. Then he tucked the bundle under his arm while he tied a quick overhand knot to secure the cord, and then he presented the barley to Arthur as though it were a bouquet of flowers.

Arthur laughed and examined Mister Hillyard's handiwork. "Very pretty," he said with a grin, and handed it back. "Now, what does this have to do with getting this whole field raked properly."

"Oh, we won't be raking it. We'll be gathering it all into these sheafs, standing them up in stooks to dry for a few weeks, and then we'll get to the threshing. As I recall, that is your favorite part, no?"

The older man's eyes twinkled, and Arthur favored him with a sour expression.

Arthur asked doubtfully, "The whole field?"

"Aye. Once you have the knack of it, it goes quickly enough. Won't take more than today and tomorrow to get it all done, I'd wager."

Arthur groaned for show, but his heart wasn't in it. In truth, he was enjoying getting to understand the operation of all the different aspects of the farm.

Amidst his conversations with Mister Hillyard, he was making his peace with the anticipation that he would wind up in farming himself, whenever his service in His Majesty's army ended. Though there seemed little prospect of doing so back home, he'd become convinced, in learning how things were done here in America, that he would be back here — whatever the outcome of the war.

He bent beside Mister Hillyard and tried to gather up a similar sheaf of barley stalks. Right away, he ran into trouble, as it seemed that half of what he'd picked up wanted to fall right back to the ground, in a confused jumble. Frowning, he mimicked Mister Hillyard's motions as best he could, though when he was done, his bundle was pathetically small and uneven in comparison.

"Not to worry, Mister Leary. Easier to practice tying it that small, anyway. Now, if you can't get a grip on the stalks you'll use to tie the rest with, you can use your mouth to hold them while you twist, like so." He demonstrated, and then wrapped the cord around his bundle, holding the loose end with the thumb that he had clamped around the bundle.

Again the bundle went under his arm as he knotted the cord, and he bent to retrieve the first one, crossing them and standing them up against each other. He held them in place and motioned to the bundle in Arthur's hand. "Need yours to hold these two up," he said, "so get along with it."

Arthur extracted a trio of stalks and tucked the end in his mouth, clamping the stalks between his teeth. He twisted them together, but as he released the cord from his mouth to wrap it around the ragged little sheaf in his hand, the three stalks sprang apart, undoing much of the twist he'd given them.

He frowned and pushed on doggedly, catching the cord under his thumb near where it was still partially twisted, and then wrapped it around the sheaf. Next, he tucked the bundle of stalks under his arm tightly and cinched the cord in a firm knot, just as Mister Hillyard had done, and finally handed over the completed sheaf.

Mister Hillyard smiled and braced his two sheaves against Arthur's, stepping back to admire their combined handiwork. "Well begun is half done," he recited, and stooped to gather his next sheaf.

By the time Constance emerged with their midday switchel, Arthur felt as though he were finally getting the hang of this task. When he and Mister Hillyard went inside for supper, they had, indeed, finished stacking up a little more than half the field.

Arthur's hands were dry and chapped, though, and covered in little scratches where the cut ends of the stalks had found skin. At the end of the day, Missus Hillyard was ready with a liniment, which she handed first to Mister Hillyard, and then to Arthur.

He didn't even really notice what they ate for supper that night, and his sleep was swift to arrive and dreamless. He appreciated that all the more, considering how often of late he'd been visited in his dreams by Jameson and the pale specters of the man's wife and baby.

In his dreams, he and Jameson had discussed questions of loyalty, duty, and friendship, and how a man could find a balance between the three.

Upon waking, Arthur never remembered the content of these conversations with a man who was as dead and gone as the philosophers whose arguments they rehearsed. However, his dreams continued to chip away at his loyalty to the Crown, and made him much more comfortable in his friendships with all three members of the Hillyard family.

When word reached the farm a few days later of a terrible battle in Pennsylvania, pitting British-allied Iroquois and Loyalists against an ill-prepared militia, leading to a disastrous loss for the Americans, Arthur felt just as shocked as his hosts. The grim detail that the Iroquois had taken hundreds of scalps had filled him with the same revulsion that he saw on Constance's face.

He bowed his head and joined in the prayers for the souls of those lost, feeling not that their deaths were a victory for the Crown, but just another cost imposed by the conflict between two rivals who were both capable of committing heinous acts.

Constance had followed him to the threshold of the kitchen door after supper and demanded of him, "Are you but feigning sympathy to the losses we suffer at the hands of your government's agents, or have your views so changed that you share in our grief?"

He looked steadily into her questioning eyes. "After what happened to my man and his family at the barracks, I came to the bitter conclusion that no side in this conflict has the right of it. Nor can any side that would impose such a terrible fate on innocents continue to have a claim to my loyalty. I grieve because you grieve, and I am sad for the lives lost, more than which side claimed those lives for its own."

She nodded slowly. "It is a difficult path that you are treading, my friend, and I esteem you greatly for taking the first steps along it."

He shrugged. "I was placed on this path by my regard for

your friendship, and by the callous disregard for the lives of a man whom I loved as a brother, and those whom he loved. It would have been a greater effort to have abandoned both of those in blind loyalty to a cause that has shown that it does not owe me any particular protection."

She had smiled, a distant expression of melancholy in her eyes. "Whatever drove you to this path, I am glad that you are on it, and that you are my friend in this time when true friendship is so difficult to rely upon." She squeezed past him and returned inside without another word.

Now, days after that conversation, watching her take her turn with the flail, Arthur was reminded again of her determination. This work was difficult, but within her capacity, and more hands would make it a lighter job, so she came out to do her part. She could just as easily have stayed inside helping her mother, but she understood that she was needed here more, so here she was.

The repetitive thump of her flail and Mister Hillyard's against the dried stalks of barley was almost soothing, and the chaff that was carried up into the air by the breeze had a delicate beauty of its own as it drifted to the ground.

After some time, Mister Hillyard signaled to Constance with his hand, and both of them ceased their movements and stepped back.

Arthur gathered up the corners of the canvas on which they'd stacked the barley, and poured it into the winnowing bucket. He spread the canvas out again with Constance's help at the far end, and then pulled a couple of new stooks of barley from the wagon, tossing them onto the canvas. Constance set her flail down and took up position with the other winnowing bucket, holding it in place as Arthur poured the barley into it, letting the breeze carry off even more of the chaff.

Unfortunately, they'd judged the wind wrong this time, and she ended up with a face full of chaff, which made her sneeze.

Her father laughed as she brushed the broken stalks and other discard parts of the barley plants out of her hair and off her face.

"It happens without fail," he said, mirth still evident in his tone. "Chaff in the wind is worse than smoke in a breeze."

Plucking a stalk out of the neck of her chemise, Constance said, ruefully, "At least smoke clears away on its own." She spat out a bit of chaff that had gotten into her mouth and glared at Arthur, as though daring him to join in her father's laughter at her expense. He maintained a straight face until she turned her back to him to finish clearing out her neckline, and then he shared a look with Mister Hillyard that caused the older man to erupt into laughter again.

Picking up her winnowing bucket, Constance smiled grimly at Arthur. "Your turn to take your chances, my amused friend."

The next stream of golden grain between the buckets yielded less chaff, and Arthur had judged the breeze correctly enough that he did not suffer the same fate as she had.

He stood with his bucket and shrugged at her. "Lucky, I guess," he said.

She shook her head, but said nothing, her own smile starting to creep out around the corners of her mouth.

They continued passing the grain back and forth between the buckets until there was almost no chaff to be separated anymore, and then Arthur poured the barley into the barrel that Mister

Hillyard had indicated when they'd started.

He glanced inside and commented, "What is that, five lots, or six? Barrel's almost half full."

"Aye, and I've more barrels clean and dry and ready to receive the barley when this one's filled." Mister Hillyard seemed satisfied, at their progress, though. He picked up his flail again, and Arthur picked up the other.

Constance said, "I'll be back out in a moment. I need to go and shake out my clothes more thoroughly in privacy."

Mister Hillyard grunted in acknowledgment as he worked the flail, and Arthur continued to master his urge to giggle at her mishap. His own flail worked at the grain in a comfortable, familiar rhythm. As much as he disliked threshing, this at least was a task that he knew how to do without much instruction.

After a short while, Constance emerged from the house and headed over to the field to pick up the next couple of stooks. Arthur followed her progress with his eyes as he continued to beat the grain. When he looked back at Mister Hillyard, the farmer was watching him with an expression of mild amusement.

Without preamble, he asked, "You fancy her, son?"

Arthur sputtered, "Wha- Oh, erm, well, she's very nice, and a hard worker, but I wouldn't dare say that I fancy her, Mister Hillyard. I am aware of my station in life, and I hardly think that someone like me is fit to dream of fancying someone like her."

Mister Hillyard, his rhythm with the flail never faltering, said, "Well, it's only that I see you watching her, and I know that you call each other friend, and so it is only natural that a father should have certain questions about what that means, and what you intend for it to mean."

Distracted, Arthur lost track of where his flail was landing, and rapped it against the other man's sharply, knocking both of their tools out of their hands.

Stooping to recover his implement, Arthur said, "I beg your pardon, both for my clumsiness, and for any misunderstanding. I presume that on some date soon, we will hear word of the end of this war, for good or for ill, and that will mark the end of my time here, as I will be obliged to return with my regiment whence we came."

Mister Hillyard nodded slowly as he bent to retrieve his own flail. "You are right, of course, and I can understand how your duty there might preclude you from making any plans beyond the end of this affair. Have you thought about what you will do after your service in the King's name?"

Arthur grimaced, not wanting to share all that was on his mind in regard to these questions. "I can't say that I have, much, no. All I know is what farming I learned as a boy — and here with you — and soldiering. There's no land that a man on a soldier's pension could dream of back home, though, so that leaves me at loose ends, unless I should make the army my life's work."

"Plenty of land here in this country," Mister Hillyard said, conversationally. "And you're a quick study on how we go about things in these parts." He shrugged. "I hope that you've been giving the matter some thought. As I said before, I'd be happy to have you as a neighbor."

Arthur was relieved at the change of subject from the question of Constance. He nodded, agreeing, "I cannot deny that this is a handsome land, what I have seen of it, and I could do far worse than to have you and your family as neighbors. The thought has occurred to me that I might find a place for myself on these shores, when the present conflict has ended," he confessed.

He sighed and added, "However, I misdoubt that all of those in these parts would be able to overlook my origins, regardless of which side prevails in the contest between our countries."

He chuckled ruefully, shaking his head. "And now you have me referring to these colonies as a different country than England. Perhaps it is just a matter of repeating the thought often enough to wear down your opponents, after all."

Mister Hillyard smiled knowingly and then turned to greet Constance as she arrived with a stook of barley on each shoulder. Arthur glance at her, and then looked at her more closely, taking note of her complexion, which had gone nearly white, and the sweat that had sprung up across her forehead. She started to say something, faltered, and fell heavily to the ground.

Chapter 17

On the kitchen table, which Mister Hillyard had carelessly cleared with an unhesitating sweep of his arm as Arthur carried his daughter through the door, Constance stirred.

Missus Hillyard murmured something into her ear, while brushing her hair back from the wet cloth that lay across her forehead. Then she looked up accusingly at her husband and Arthur, hissing, "Working her like a mule in this heat, it's no wonder that she fainted."

Constance protested weakly, "No, Mama, they asked less of me than of themselves." She gathered her strength for a moment and added, "It is only that it is a warm day, and I am obliged to wear all of these petticoats and skirts. They may dress more sensibly for the weather, which is not their doing."

Missus Hillyard frowned fiercely. "Well, we'll have no more of you playing at doing a man's work, in any event."

"But Mama, there's too much for just two people. Some of the tasks require more hands."

Arthur could see from the set of Missus Hillyard's mouth that this was not an argument that the younger woman was going to win.

He spoke up, saying, "Nay, do not worry, Constance. We will manage, and your well-being is more important in any event."

She pushed herself up on her elbows and fixed Arthur with a glare. "Arthur Leary, I am perfectly able to look after my own well-being, thank you very much."

Mister Hillyard headed off the brewing argument, interjecting, "Be that as it may, Constance, Mister Leary is right. We will manage with just the two of us. Your help was greatly appreciated, but we haven't yet even reached the heat of the day, and as you pointed out, your attire is not well-suited to doing heavy work under these conditions."

He turned to his wife and said, "See that she takes her ease for the rest of the afternoon. There's no sense in taking any chances of her falling in a faint twice in one day."

Constance's expression had gone from obstinate to outright stormy, and Arthur braced himself for the explosion that was obviously imminent.

Instead, he watched her take a deep breath, control her temper, and say in a tight, even voice, "Very well, Papa. I will rest, but only because I find that I still do not have my strength. If the work is not done tomorrow, I will join you again."

Mister Hillyard exchanged a glance with Arthur, and it was clear that they both understood that whatever it took, the threshing would be finished today. However, to his daughter, the farmer simply said, "Of course, dear. Now, do you need help to get upstairs to your bed?"

Once Constance was settled down, the two men returned to the seemingly endless routine of threshing, winnowing, and storing the barley, and then getting more stooks from the field. By the time the sun was low on the horizon and Missus Hillyard had come out to call them to supper for the second time, they were just winnowing the last round.

Supper was punctuated by Arthur falling asleep in his seat for a moment between the boiled pudding and the soup, much to everyone's entertainment but his own. He excused himself and collapsed on his pallet in his quarters as soon as it was decent, and was aware of nothing until Constance knocked on his door with his breakfast in the morning.

Blinking sleepily and sitting up, he called out, "Come in."

She entered with his customary porridge and cider, which she set on his table. She straightened and said, quietly, "You and Papa did not need to labor so hard yesterday, just to spare me from helping again today."

He nodded, still bleary and no more than half awake. "I know that, but we agreed that it would be best for you to relax a bit today, and ensure that you are completely recovered."

She scowled, and then her expression softened ever so slightly into a frown. "In truth, I've not been feeling completely myself for several days now. Mama's been dosing me with all manner of tinctures to try to settle my stomach, but nothing's really been working."

Alarmed now, Arthur arose from his pallet, approaching her. "Do you feel otherwise well?"

She laughed lightly. "Once I am sick after I rise and get it out of the way, I am usually fine the rest of the day, but it's still a nuisance. In any event, it should not have been cause for you and Papa to work so hard yesterday."

Arthur took her hands in his, struck anew at just how small and fine-boned they were in comparison to his own. "I would do it again, to spare you from another spell of fainting — or worse."

She smiled and looked away, seemingly bashful, but she did not pull her hands from his grasp. Turning back to face him, she smiled brightly. "Well, it just leaves me free to complete my chores in the barn today, so I shall still find a way to earn my keep."

He returned her smile and shook his head ruefully. "Thank you for bringing me my breakfast, Constance."

"You are most welcome, Arthur. After you've finished, bring the plate in to Mama, and I'll get started on my work before it gets hot."

He nodded and sat down to eat. He didn't really even taste the food, he was still so tired, but when it was done, he dutifully brought the plate inside. Missus Hillyard was in the kitchen as usual, but Mister Hillyard was there, as well, sitting at the table with a serious expression on his face.

As Arthur handed the plate to Missus Hillyard, her husband said, "Sit down, son. There's a matter we need to discuss with you."

Arthur's blood ran cold at these words, but he complied, and Missus Hillyard joined her husband on the other side of the table.

The farmer spoke first. "Mister Leary, you've proved yourself a hard worker, and a capable learner in the time you've been here. Missus Hillyard and I have been pleased to see your willingness to do more than merely what is asked of you, and to apply yourself to doing as creditable a job as you're capable of in every task we have set you to."

"Why, thank you, Mister Hillyard, Missus Hillyard. I guess it never would have occurred to me to do otherwise."

"Well, you would be surprised at the sort of excuses some laborers we have seen will offer in place of honest work. It was a stroke of good fortune that I thought to bid on your hire, and I wanted you to know that your efforts here have not gone without notice."

"Thank you," Arthur repeated, unsure what else he could say.

"Now, I know that you and our daughter have developed a good understanding, despite your differences in background and even beliefs, and have become valued friends to one another."

Arthur's head was spinning at the rapid change in subjects. What did the one have to do with the other? Outwardly, though, he just blinked and said, "Why, yes, she and I have come to an understanding about the differences in our outlooks." He smiled ruefully. "If nothing else, she is a lively conversationalist, and a capable and determined help with work when I must call upon her."

Mister Hillyard nodded. "Aye, that she is, even to her own detriment, as we saw yesterday. Now, you and I talked not long ago about your plans after the war, and you said that you'd like to someday have a farm of your own."

Once again, the course of the conversation was going in seemingly random directions, though the way that Missus Hillyard gripped her husband's hand, it seemed as though there was some reason to it that she was well aware of. "Well, aye, when my duties to my regiment have been satisfied, I believe that I should like that well enough, yes."

"As we also discussed, your prospects of getting a farm back in England are dim, so you mentioned that you might well wind up back on these shores — whether we are yet a colony under the King's thumb, or an independent nation — if only because land is the one thing that we have in boundless abundance."

Hesitantly now, Arthur answered, "Aye, though there are other places under the King's dominion that also offer the possibility of land grants, should General Washington prevail in the end."

Mister Hillyard nodded, although his attention didn't really seem to be on what Arthur was saying, but rather on what he was planning to say next. The farmer took a deep breath and looked to his wife for reassurance. She met his eyes and gave him a quick nod, and Mister Hillyard plunged on.

"It's like this, Mister Leary. Missus Hillyard is quite certain that that accursed Contant has got our daughter with child, and we should like for you to marry her and save the baby from being born a bastard."

Arthur's ears roared, and he shook his head violently, as though he were a plow-horse bedeviled with flies. "Come again, would you? You're asking me to abandon my regiment, stay here, and marry your daughter?"

Mister Hillyard looked grave and he nodded. "Aye, that I am. And in the fullness of time, this farm will pass into your name, should you do so. You'll be a man of substance, with a worthy partner at your side. Your concerns that Constance deserves someone whose station in life is equal to her own will be resolved at one stroke."

Arthur raised his index finger, which seemed at the moment to be the only motion he could muster. "And what does Constance think about this?"

Mister Hillyard waved his hand dismissively. "You fancy

her, and unless we misunderstand our daughter greatly, she fancies you well enough, which is more than Missus Hillyard and I had when we married"

He chuckled. "Missus Hillyard had only clapped eyes on me for the first time a fortnight before our wedding day, and her father pointed me out to her, telling her that he was going to try to get me to marry her." He grinned. "I wasn't that hard to convince, once he showed me this beautiful parcel, and I got to know her a little bit."

Missus Hillyard shot her husband a look and spoke up for the first time since Arthur had come into the kitchen. "Constance speaks very highly of you, my dear, and holds you in great esteem. I know that you'll take care of her, and make her much happier than that awful Contant boy ever did."

Arthur frowned. "And what happens when my regiment gets its orders to return home to England, or moves to some distant location, either under orders from your armies, or on its own initiative, as the case may be? Will you be satisfied for her to follow me wherever my duty may take me?"

Mister Hillyard frowned. "I will confess I had hoped that you would simply stay. I spoke to one of my neighbors in the area here who likewise secured the labor of one of your number at the Cambridge barracks, and when that man married his neighbor's daughter, he was released from service."

The farmer pursed his lips thoughtfully. "I do not know if his release was through a recognized means or was more irregular, but I was given to understand that you were less than charmed with certain aspects of your officers' care for the well-being of your men and their parties, so I thought . . ." He trailed off delicately, and Arthur scowled.

"You thought that I might simply desert, and renege on the duties I owe to my regiment and my King?"

Mister Hillyard made a placating motion with his hands. Clearly, this conversation had taken a turn that he had not anticipated, and was not entirely comfortable with. Arthur took a deep breath, closing his eyes to think for a moment.

Marry Constance, and play the part of a father to the cuckoo's egg? Save Constance from the shame of her presumed circumstance? Abandon an army that seemed destined to only to shrivel away into irrelevance and disease, and which seemed unlikely to ever actually return home? Accept a prospective inheritance that would secure his position in society for his life? Spend that life alongside Constance?

He opened his eyes and found both Mister and Missus Hillyard watching him closely. He nodded once, decisively. "If she'll have me, I will do it."

Chapter 18

It was not the answer that Arthur expected to the most important question he had ever asked. Constance's eyes narrowed, and she asked, suspiciously, "Are you practicing at making a fool of me? Did my father put you up to this? Why is he so determined to see me married off?"

"No, Constance, let me explain!" Arthur called after her as she whirled and marched away toward the house, head held high and back ramrod-straight, but she did not so much as acknowledge that she had heard him. He followed her to the house, but she slammed the kitchen door in his face and shot the bolt, leaving him locked out and with no option but to return to his own quarters.

Through the walls of the house, though, he could hear her confronting her father, and he paused shamelessly to listen in, his heart still pounding from having worked up the nerve to pose the question to her in the first place.

Constance's voice was clearly audible as she demanded, "What business is it of yours whether or when I am married? Have you learned nothing at all from the disaster of the last boy you tried to throw me at?"

Arthur could not make out her father's reply, but it clearly did not mollify his daughter.

"Did you forget that he has sworn an oath to support the same Crown that sent him here to slaughter our militiamen? Have you forgotten Frederick so soon?" Arthur froze. This was a name he had never heard mentioned.

This time, he could make out a few words of Mister Hillyard's answer. ". . . never forget Frederick, but you seem to have forgot that you cannot wed a man who has been dead for a year and more." Arthur's blood ran cold. Had Constance been betrothed before her ill-fated courtship with Mister Contant? How had he missed hearing about this until now?

Clearly infuriated at her father's disregard for the matters of her heart, Constance lifted her voice rose to nearly a banshee's shriek, and Arthur cringed, imagining how piercing it must be within the confines of the kitchen.

"I know full well that I cannot wed him, and it could easily have been your precious Mister Leary who stole him away from me!"

Mister Hillyard interjected something inaudible, and she replied, "I know that they were not at the same place, but this man was sent here to kill our men — he has admitted to me that he knows he has killed at least one — and you cannot simply overlook that fact."

Arthur was glad that Mister Hillyard's next words were as clear and firm as though he were in the room with them, and was warmed by what the man said.

"Mister Leary is a good man, Constance, and a clever and industrious worker. If you will permit him to do so, he will make you a fine and honorable husband." He paused, and then added, "Your mother is quite certain that you will be needing one in just a few month's time, my daughter."

Arthur could almost feel Constance's shocked silence as a

presence emanating from the house, and then she asked something that he could not make out. Her father answered, "Yes, my dear, your mother sees all of the signs, and she tells me that you missed your courses this month, to boot."

Constance did not answer in words, but her sob drove Arthur to quit the side of the house where he had been eavesdropping, to return to his own quarters.

The revelation that Constance had been betrothed had shaken him, and that her intended had been killed in battle did much to explain her hostility to the Crown, and even her initial reserved attitude toward him.

Seen in that light, her rejection of his suit just now was not only understandable, but it seemed almost inevitable. He could hardly imagine any circumstance that would enable a woman to overcome the resentment against the nation that had murdered the man she thought she was going to marry. And after he had confessed to having taken the life of one of her betrothed's fellow soldiers . . . why, he was surprised that she had not spat in his face immediately, not to mention daily thereafter.

Arthur sank down and curled up on his pallet, wishing that Mister Hillyard or his wife had been more forthcoming about this factor when they suggested that he should marry their daughter. It seemed to him to be a rather critical fact to have omitted.

He found himself thinking back to every conversation he'd had with Constance, trying to remember when she had first seen him not as a killer of men such as her fiancé, but as an individual with whom she might find friendship. And at which points in their discussions had that thought been lurking in the back of her mind, festering and whispering additions to the things he said?

They had never again discussed the battles Arthur had seen, nor had he been particularly keen to do so even before learning this new fact about her. Now, how could they ever even broach the subject without the thought hanging in the air like the burst of a lost egg gone bad, befouling everything it could reach?

"Tell me, how many times have you shot at an American soldier?"

"I have no count, and I may have hit them on many occasions aside from the one I related to you."

"Did it occur to you to think that they may have had mothers who would weep for them, fathers who would grieve in silence, sweethearts whose hearts would never mend?"

"Nay, in truth it did not, for they were simply my enemy, and in order to strive against one another, we all needed to set aside that knowledge, else we would all have laid down our arms and retired from the field, leaving the contest forever undecided."

"Is it not undecided yet, even with the blood spilled on both sides?"

Arthur could picture the exchange as clearly in his mind as though it had happened, and he could see, as well, that there was no way he could make her understand or forgive his past.

For that matter, in this moment, neither could he understand or forgive it himself.

There was a soft knock at the door, and Constance entered before he could even answer. Her eyes were puffy and rimmed in red, and bright with the tears that threatened to spill again.

She said, "Mama sent me to tell you that supper is ready, but first, there are some things that I would say to you."

He nodded and stood, preferring to meet his fate on his

feet.

"Papa has explained to me that it is likely that I bear Mister Contant's baby." She reached down and almost unconsciously cupped her hand over her belly. "I was innocent of this information when you spoke to me earlier, and it explains, at least, why Papa pressed you to propose marriage to me."

Arthur interjected, quietly but firmly, "I was not unwilling, as you are a better woman than I could hope to deserve."

Constance shook her head dismissively. "There is much that you do not know about me, Arthur, and that may change your opinion of me."

Arthur tried to speak, but she raised a hand to silence him, and continued, "In addition to having been despoiled by Mister Contant, years before your arrival on this farm, my heart was lost to another . . . and then destroyed by his loss."

A tear trickled down her cheek, but she sniffed hard and forced herself to continue. "His name was Frederick Baker, and he was a volunteer with a regiment that was fighting in New-Jersey when he was struck down. He had asked me to marry him before he departed, and though I had accepted his suit, we both decided that it was best to wait until he was released from his service, rather than try to find some way for me to follow him — or to be left here as his wife in name only."

She let her chin fall to her chest, and Arthur could see her biting her lip in a vain attempt to gain control over the tears that spilled down her cheeks now. She angrily swiped them away with her hands and lifted her chin. "When the news reached us that he was lost, I refused to believe it. I do think Mama and Papa were afraid that I had lost my senses entirely."

She smiled wanly. "Although Papa may have dreamed of seeing this farm enlarged by the addition of Mister Contant's parcel, in truth, he wanted even more for my heart to find some new safe haven."

She sighed heavily. "And now, with Mister Contant first proved false and unworthy and then gone without a trace, Papa thought to suggest you as a possible substitution to him, instead of accepting that his daughter's heart might simply be unhealed for all time."

She started weeping openly then, and Arthur could bear it no more. He stepped forward and pulled her into his arms. She stiffened at first, but then relaxed into him, and he stood just holding her until her shoulders stopped quaking. Eventually, she sniffled and pulled away, murmuring, "We should go in for supper."

He nodded, but kept his hands on her shoulders for a moment, his eyes roving over her face. "Unhealed or not, your heart is the truest I've known, and no loss is too great to bear for the spirit that I see in you."

Though he'd started saying the words at first to offer her some comfort, as they emerged, he could feel the truth in them fall into place in his own mind.

She leaned into his embrace once more, but this time, it felt different.

When her breathing calmed, she finally looked up at him. Almost inaudibly, she said, "Thank you, Arthur. Knowing what you know about me now, and knowing that coming to trust you will demand the utmost effort from us both, if you'll still have me, my answer is yes."

Chapter 19

Mister Hillyard stood from his pew in the small church, and spoke in a clear, strong voice, "I hereby declare the banns of marriage between Constance Hillyard and Arthur Leary. This is the first time of asking. If any of you know cause or just impediment why these two people should not be joined together in holy matrimony, ye are to declare it."

He looked around at the congregation, and Arthur could see his eye light upon Mister Contant. It seemed incredible in light of all that had passed between the families that Jack's father might be present at the church, and Arthur noticed that Mister Hillyard's eyes narrowed as he looked at the man.

Mister Contant tightened his mouth into a grimace, but said nothing, so Mister Hillyard swung his gaze back to the priest at the front of the church. The priest paused for a moment longer, nodded, and intoned, "The banns of marriage between Constance Hillyard and Arthur Leary have been declared and published for the first time. Should there be nobody who declares any just impediment to their union after the third declaration of the banns, they shall be wed as soon as it is convenient for them both."

In the pew, Constance's hand tightened around Arthur's, and he returned the squeeze. The rest of the service flowed past in a series of other community announcements, a homily from the priest, and then came an item that perked Arthur's ears up, and he paid rapt attention.

"We have received word of a decisive victory by his Excellency General George Washington against the forces of the British grand army under the command of their General Clinton as they attempted to complete their flight from Philadelphia by sea. Despite their having suffered a withering attack at the beginning of the battle, General Washington personally rallied the American forces at a place called Monmouth, New-Jersey, and left the British no choice but to retreat from the field, leaving behind their dead and wounded."

He looked out over the congregation, his expression determined and serious. "I would ask that you join me in prayer for the continued success of our esteemed General Washington, and for the safety of his men in their efforts to throw of the yoke of the British Crown."

The priest bent his head, and Arthur, whatever his misgivings, knew that to do other than to join the congregation in following his lead would be a bad idea. He was unsurprised that General Clinton had again been involved in a debacle for the British forces.

At first, he did not appeal to God on Washington's behalf, but neither did he find that he could ask the great Author of the world for His intercession on the behalf of the British side, particularly Clinton. The sacrifices he had heard of and witnessed of these people, and their industry in making their way in this country, those had merit as well.

And then, of course, there was also the matter of Constance, who small, warm hand within his was a reminder that he had committed to bind himself to the fate of this family — and their country — and so it would be no more than sensible for him to pray for Washington to prevail against his countrymen, and his fellow soldiers in arms under the banner of the British Crown. If it meant that Clinton would be exposed for the bumbler he was, so much the better. Still, he could not bring himself to ask God for the defeat of his fellow soldiers — on either side, he realized with a start. He sighed inwardly and settled on asking only mercy for the souls lost, and peace for those who yet fought. Would that a peace could be concluded before any more men had to sleep under the soil of this country!

That was up to the men in London, though, and wherever the American's Congress now met. As with all wars throughout history, those who carried the sword had little voice in how they must direct its strike, but could only hope for the good fortune of being under competent leaders — at all levels.

He was brought out of these bitter thoughts when Constance squeezed his hand to alert him that it was time to stand and sing. As with all church services he'd attended, he didn't know the music, but there were enough in the pews around him who did that he could move his mouth in silence without being caught out.

Constance noticed, of course, and he saw her mouth twitch in a half-smile between verses. He glanced at her and smiled back, shaking his head ruefully.

After the service was over, they had just left the small church when Mister Contant approached the family, his hands clasped behind his back and his mouth still set in a deep grimace. He addressed himself to Mister Hillyard.

"Gregory, eh, a word?" Mister Hillyard turned and regarded the man. Arthur felt Constance's hand clench tightly around his, and he drew her closer, putting his arm around her protectively.

Stiffly, Mister Hillyard replied, "We have already exchanged some words, Mister Contant. Have you some new ones to offer?"

"I might, at that," Contant said, his voice cold and flat. "My boy is gone, and I salute you for having the wit to make it look as though he was taken by an animal."

Mister Hillyard's eyes narrowed. "Are you accusing me of murder, in front of this congregation of our neighbors and friends?"

"Nay, as I said, you were canny enough to make it believable that you bore no responsibility."

Mister Hillyard stepped toward the other man, who stumbled back in surprise. "Mister Contant, your boy was foolish enough to go alone into the woods, or perhaps he had no friends left who were willing to suffer his company. Whatever the case may be, he alone is responsible for what happened to him. If you want to fix blame on anyone else but your son, I suggest that you look to the nearest mirror."

Missus Hillyard took her husband by the elbow. "We had best be going, Mister Hillyard. The afternoon is getting on."

"True enough, my dear," her husband replied, and waved at someone in the slowly-dispersing congregation who had waved to him. "We had best be getting home, as there are chores that need doing before sundown. We wouldn't want to be caught out of doors when there are dangerous animals about."

Mister Contant's eyes flashed dangerously, but he said nothing, spitting on the ground beside Arthur's feet and stomping away. The members of the congregation followed his progress away from the church with expressions that ranged from open hostility to careful neutrality.

Mister Hillyard bowed his farewell to the priest, and accepted the congratulations of many in the congregation, before he was able to lead his family away and back to their farm.

After supper that evening, Arthur retired to his quarters, where he laid awake for some time, petting the grey cat curled up alongside him, and pondering the question of loyalty. General Burgoyne's convention — how long had it been since he'd thought of that? — meant that he would likely not ever again been asked take up arms against the American cause, anyway.

And his new obligations, as Constance's betrothed, as well as his residual uncertainty about the cause of independence from the Crown, ruled out his taking up arms for the American side. Loyalty had been purely an exercise for the intellect for some time — so why did it vex him so?

He'd found no satisfactory answers by the time sleep claimed him, although he had concluded that there was little to lose by simply giving the outward appearances of support for American independence — and who knew, perhaps he would eventually find that he truly did support their cause.

There came then a golden string of days, each following in the pattern of the one before it. Whether awakened by the rooster or by Constance bringing his breakfast each morning, Arthur rose early and enjoyed a brief conversation with her as he ate, each discussion reinforcing his opinion of her lively intellect and strength of character.

She was coming to trust his embrace more with each passing day, though she still admitted difficulty at times.

"I can tell myself that you are not him, and your touch should not bring me any alarm, but my heart clenches just a little bit until I can reassure it."

He murmured into her hair, "I only hope that in time, I can reassure your heart, too."

He'd come to crave the moments when they shared a hug before each started in on their chores of the day. She felt fragile in his arms, but he reminded himself that she was probably more resilient than he. She was also warm in the morning chill, and on days that were particularly cool from the prior night, it seemed to him that she was most likely to stand near him as he ate.

For his part, he was becoming more comfortable with his place in the family. Mister Hillyard said that once they were wed, he would move into the house — at least, until they could build a second house on the property for the young family — but in the meantime, propriety required that he remain in his quarters.

However, Arthur's work in the myriad of tasks involved in managing the farm had changed in its tenor. Mister Hillyard had shifted from instructing him on just the rote motions he must go through as a hired laborer, to explaining the rationale of everything he did, as a future master of the farm.

The barley, for example, that they had so painstakingly dried and threshed, they were now engaged in malting — a process that required that the carefully dried grain be wetted until it sprouted, and then immediately dried and heated to stop the growth and prepare it for Missus Hillyard's kitchen.

Where Mister Hillyard would previously have simply told Arthur what to do, he now explained that they were taking these pains in order to ensure that the ale that Missus Hillyard would make from it would produce the best flavor, and keep as well as possible through the winter months.

"Letting it sprout changes the flavor from tasting like flour to tasting just sweet, like the sap of a birch tree in springtime. Stopping it from growing and heating it to just the right point preserves that sweetness, and readies the barley for the brewing kettle. If you do any part of it incorrectly, the ale tastes off, does not refresh, and does not keep."

"And Constance knows Missus Hillyard's methods?"

"Oh, aye, she's been helping her mother with the brewing since she was a little girl, to one extent or another."

Mister Hillyard gave Arthur a friendly nudge with his elbow. "Never fear, she will know how to keep you supplied with ale when she is your wife, without you having to resort to buying from some ale-wife."

He handed the rake he was using to turn the barley on the broad tin pan over a bed of low coals to Arthur. "Here, have a feel of this. The grains of malt are about done drying and toasting, and I want you to have a sense of how they move about in the pan when they reach this point. Notice how they pass through the rake easily, without clumping together in the slightest. That's what you are looking for."

Arthur did as directed, and found that he enjoyed the relaxing sight of the golden, almost copper-colored grains as they flowed through the rake. He nodded. "They have a beauty of their own, don't they? Quite apart from their utility in making a healthful drink for us, they are lovely to behold."

Mister Hillyard smiled. "That they are, yes. Let's get this pan tipped into the barrel and start up the next one."

They passed the rest of the afternoon finishing that chore, and after the last pan of malt was put into its barrel, and the last bed of coals was banked and wetted down, Mister Hillyard closed up the barrel.

"We're not going to seal this for long-term storage, as we've been out of ale for a while now. So, Missus Hillyard will be using it within the month, most likely, and we need only set the head in place and tighten the staves."

As he spoke, he illustrated what he meant by dropping the lid down inside the barrel, then catching the edge of it in the groove around the top of the inside and lifting it into place with a long, hooked tool.

Walking around the barrel with a hammer and a blunt chisel-like tool, he drove the loosened hoops down the side until they gripped tight, one after the next.

"Just need to make sure that this is in the groove all the way around —" he illustrated by running his fingers around the perimeter of the lid " — and then we'll tap this top hoop into place."

He handed the hammer to Arthur. "Just run this around the top of the barrel, to drive the hoop down even with the staves. Missus Hillyard might need help prying it off, but we don't want the head popping off while we move the barrel around."

Arthur took the hammer and tapped the iron hoop down as he was told, mimicking Mister Hillyard's practice of moving the tool around the top of barrel in order to get the hoop evenly placed.

The older man nodded approvingly. "One would think that you'd apprenticed with a cooper, that was so neatly done. Let's get this rolled into the barn, and then we can check on Gertie."

Gertie had been bred to a neighbor's bull well before Arthur's arrival, and was due for calving any day now. Missus Hillyard had mentioned on several occasions that she was eager for Gertie's milk to come in, as their other cow was taken ill and died suddenly the prior summer. She'd once said wistfully, "We've had no new cheese or milk but what we could buy for a year now."

"I hope Gertie gives us another cow, but if it's a bull, the meat will be nice, too," Mister Hillyard remarked as he entered the cow's stall, stroking her side to let her know where he was. "She's a good old girl. Her first calf was a bull, and though Gertie did a fine job of raising him, we had a difficult time of things when it came time to slaughter him for the table."

"Gertie gave you trouble over losing her calf?"

Mister Hillyard uttered a brief chuckle. "Nay, it was your Constance who raised a fuss. Named the thing Tommy, she had, even though we told her that we don't name food. She was old enough to know better, but she just couldn't help herself."

He gave Arthur a quick smile. "She'll be your trouble in a couple of weeks, so it's best that you know her failings, what few there are. She is too kind-hearted when it comes to animals she's seen raised, even though she is avid about enjoying meat when it's on the table before her. She is too much inclined to bear difficulties long past where they should be endured, so mind that you don't add to her burdens unnecessarily."

Mister Hillyard got a distant look in his eye, and his smile turned gentle. "She is much like her mother was at that age in her determination to do her part and more, but as she is so much smaller than even Missus Hillyard was, she is likely to take on too much. You will have your hands full, trying to keep her from her chores as her time approaches."

Arthur grinned. "I should think that it would be more productive to let her learn of the hazards from some friend who has preceded her in childbirth. When my brother's wife was with child, her friends told her stories that would raise the hair on the back of your neck, and the poor woman scarcely dared to rise from her bed."

Mister Hillyard grinned in reply, wagging a finger at him. "You've had the advantage of seeing others before you demonstrate how to manage a peaceable marriage."

Arthur shook his head, his own smile becoming more thoughtful. "Oh, I wish that Jacob's marriage was all that peaceable, but I very much doubt that Constance is half as spirited as his Theresa turned out to be. At least, I hope not. The last letter I had of him, she had run off for a time, but had just returned, somewhat chastened by some misadventures."

He shrugged. "Well, that's how Jacob told it. Having grown up with him, I have reason to suspect that he may have given her cause to take her leave, and *that* much of his example, I can say that I have profited by having witnessed. I know better what not to do as a result."

Mister Hillyard laughed again, and gave Gertie an affectionate pat on the flank as he finished his examination of her. "Well, Gertie's still going to be a while yet, it looks like, so you and I can get cleaned up and see where supper stands."

Chapter 20

If Constance had been lovely when he'd first seen her, today she was breathtaking. Arthur stole another glance over at her as they rode together in the back of the wagon on their way to the meeting-house for their wedding ceremony. She caught him looking at her, and smiled at him with a bit of a twinkle in her eye.

He'd never seen her wear the deep blue dress before, but he thought that the color suited her perfectly, and the cut of it somehow made her look taller and less fragile than his first impression of her had been. If he had his way, she would have more than one dress in this shade, once they were prosperous enough. The crisp white cap she wore looked as though it were newly-made, crowning her head in a way that seemed to hold her entire spine straight and proud.

As for himself, he wore a shirt that Mister Hillyard had gifted him, decorated with a fashionable ruffle at the chest, and topped with a fresh white stock about his neck. A borrowed waistcoat and a new cocked hat completed his transformation in appearance from an English-farmer-turned-soldier into an American-farmer-turned-groom.

The cart bumped down the road, and Constance was jostled into him from time to time as it struck rocks and ruts left from another vicious thunderstorm the prior week.

Of course, Gertie had chosen that stormy night to calve,

and both Mister Hillyard and Arthur had been drenched by the time they delivered the new calf — a heifer, offering the promise of milk in the years ahead, in addition to what immediate supply her mother could spare.

After the birth was over, Arthur had spent the evening warming and drying himself before the kitchen hearth beside Mister Hillyard, while Constance and Missus Hillyard brought them both warm drinks and warmer praise, restoring them from their misery into a state of comfort.

Constance had snuck a kiss onto Arthur's lips while her mother was busy rubbing warmth into Mister Hillyard's hands, and her parents' attention was on each other. The memory of that brief contact had sustained Arthur through the interminable wait for the third declaration of the banns.

Now, with the event at hand, he found that he was eager to repeat that kiss, and more, once the celebrations were over. He looked over at her and found her gazing at him, though her eyes darted nervously away when she saw that she'd been caught. He gave her hand a squeeze, and she smiled at him again, seeming abashed at having been so jumpy.

Before leaving the house, Mister Hillyard had been apologetic at how meager the wedding feast would be. "In the times before these troubles, we would have had people from all the country around out to the house to toast your union, and we would probably have still been at it after three days' time."

He sighed. "Now, though, as things are, we'll have a few friends out to eat the meal that Missus Hillyard and Constance have prepared, and then we'll be back to our chores." He chuckled to himself, adding, "Although, perhaps, it is better that we live in such times, as you need not fear that any party crashers will come and try to steal Constance away tonight."

Constance's smile had frozen at that comment, and her father took note immediately. "Of course, given the circumstances, I think that the young men of the area would have been put on notice that the old practice could be passed over, so as to avoid giving the bride any undue fright."

Constance's expression turned to one of disapproval. "I never thought that a bride ought to have been subject to such disreputable treatment anyway."

Her father's mouth quirked in a half-smile. "Oh, when they came and took your mother away, they permitted me to ransom her at the price of a bottle of wine." He turned and smiled at Missus Hillyard affectionately. "She was well worth the ransom, too."

Missus Hillyard and her daughter both sniffed their disapproval in unison, and Arthur had to stifle a laugh, even though he understood Constance's particular aversion to being so treated.

Mister Hillyard grinned. "In any event, folk don't much do that anymore, even before this war started. And I've made sure that the word's gone around that our family has no further appetite for any resurrection of the old traditions, either."

Constance's frown softened slightly. "Thank you for that much, at least." She took a deep breath, and then blew it out gustily. "Arthur, are you as nervous as I am?"

Arthur gave a small laugh. "I reckon that I am, yes. I just keep telling myself that nobody is going to shoot at me today, and I am not about to be asked to partake in a bayonet charge." He shrugged.

Mister Hillyard had leaned toward him and mock-whispered, "You may wish for that before the day's out, son. Marriage changes your life like nothing else, and you can never know what that change will look like."

He glanced over at his daughter and added, "Of course, your Constance will be as fine a partner as her mother and I could contrive to raise her to be, so you should have aught to worry on. Come, 'tis time to go to the ceremony!"

Arthur smiled now, remembering Mister Hillyard's comment, as he gazed openly at his bride. The meeting-house hove into sight, and he was only able to quiet the wild beating of his heart within its cage of ribs by focusing on Constance.

She was not only lovely to look at, but he was sure her less-visible qualities would serve their partnership in good stead over the many years to come. Despite his having survived battlefields and privation, he was quite certain that she was more resilient than he was, and he knew from having shared the work around the farm that she worked at least as hard as he did.

More than that, though, she was wiser than he in her ability to understand that his friendship was a matter between just two people, while he'd struggled for far too long over the question of whether he could separate her identity from her nation.

As he thought about that fact, he saw with a nearly blinding flash of insight that he needed neither to separate or conjoin her identity and that of her nation in order to love both. All of his wrangling with Jameson's ghost in his dreams, the hours of pondering the philosophical questions of duties owed, and obligations to be met, vanished in a breath.

He had been asking himself the wrong questions, he realized. The scope of his obligations in this world was both more finite and unending than the simple matter of whose orders he ought follow. He needed no orders to know his place in the world; his heart alone could guide him.

It was at that instant, sitting in the back of a wagon beside Constance within sight of the meeting-house where they were to be wed, that he realized that his loyalty was only to her and their child, and that no lieutenant, general, or king could ever again command him.

Chapter 21

The messenger shivered slightly at the front door, and the wind blew in a chill gust that reached as far as the kitchen, where Arthur and Constance sat. Mister Hillyard's voice could be heard clearly through the house.

"What business brings you out on such a terrible day?"

"I've orders for a Corporal Arthur Leary, whose labor contract you bid in the spring. The Convention Army is being removed to Virginia, and he is to accompany me back to the barracks to prepare for their departure thence."

Arthur froze at the messenger's high, clear voice, as he delivered the terrible news. Constance clutched his hand from across the table, and they listened together as Mister Hillyard answered the man, his voice rumbling through the house.

"Ah, yes, Mister Leary. I've a mind to come and demand a refund from the clark who permitted me to bid on his contract. He seemed as though he was going to be a fine addition to the farm, but it took him but a few weeks to change his colors, and I've not seen any sign of the British soldier on my property in many months."

The dismay in the messenger's voice was plain. "He's deserted, then? Do you have any idea how many of those blasted soldiers took to the hills just as soon as they were out of sight of the barracks? Why, there must be a thousand of them just within a loud shout of where we stand, and the dear Lord alone knows how many of them have snuck back into the British lines."

"I am sorry to hear of your troubles, but I have my own difficulties, what with trying to manage a farm, and my only daughter married away this summer, so it's just my wife and I. We had hoped that hiring one of those prisoners would let us get by, and instead, he only brought more confusion and suspicion on our house. I'll have you know, hiring a prisoner for labor was not popular in this community."

Arthur could barely contain himself as he listened to Mister Hillyard's continued performance.

"Why, I've one neighbor who moved away completely, abandoned his parcel, and I've received word that I may be permitted to take over his grant so long as I can work it. So I'll need to hire even more men in the spring — and now you tell me that the barracks are being emptied, so I'll have to compete with the militia companies for hands, and no laborers to hire from you lot, either?"

"I am sorry to hear of your complicated fortunes, sir, but I assure you that we did not anticipate that so many of these soldiers would feel themselves to be unbound from the commitments that General Burgoyne made on their behalf."

Mister Hillyard snorted. "A man's word is his own to give, and not any other person's. Isn't that a part of what underlies this entire contest for independence?"

The messenger sighed, and Arthur almost felt sorry for him. "I suppose so, sir. I've several more hired-out prisoners to collect still before I can return home, so I'll take your leave now, if I may."

"Of course, and I wish you better fortune than I was able to provide you."

The Convention

"Thank you sir. Good day." The sound of the door closing made Arthur jump slightly, and Constance again squeezed his hand.

Mister Hillyard walked into the kitchen, a grin plastered across his face. "Well, that ought to put an end to their interest in you, son." He looked Arthur over. "You don't much answer to the description on their rolls anymore, either. Missus Hillyard's done a fine job of feeding you up, and as for your build, I don't suppose that the work in the fields here is much like that of marching."

He nodded with satisfaction. "I think you'll pass as an American."

Arthur nodded in reply and squeezed Constance's hand. "That I think I will, sir."

Also in Audiobook

Many readers love the experience of turning the pages in a paper book such as the one you hold in your hands. Others enjoy hearing a skilled narrator tell them a story, bringing the words on the page to life.

Brief Candle Press has arranged to have *The Convention* produced as a high-quality audiobook, and you can listen to a sample and learn where to purchase it in that form by scanning the QR code below with your phone, tablet, or other device, or going to the Web address shown.

Happy listening!

bit.ly/TheConventionAudio

Historical Notes

The incredible story of what happened after the British surrender at Saratoga is one that is nearly entirely overlooked in our classroom histories of the American Revolution. When I stumbled across a reference to the "Convention Army" while researching another book about prisoners of war (*The Mine*), I could not believe the details of it, which I've only been able to give the most superficial of treatment in this novel.

After being given assurance by the American General Gates that they could depart American shores just as soon as transport could be arranged, Burgoyne's captured army was delayed in Cambridge by a series of questionable maneuvers on the part of the Congress (which had not been consulted on the terms of the surrender to which Gates had agreed).

Then, as mentioned in the narrative of this book, Congress insisted that the convention of surrender be ratified by King George. Congress knew full well that the King would never take up the matter at all, as that would require that he recognize the American Congress as a legitimate governing body over what he held to be no more than colonies in a state of rebellion.

The result of this legalistic stalemate fell upon the shoulders of the British and German troops who'd been captured at Saratoga. General Burgoyne and several other senior officers were able to arrange to be exchanged, but the rank and file, as well as their wives and children and others among the camp followers, were to spend the rest of the war in American custody.

Naturally, there were substantial desertions, and in addition to deaths on the battlefield and from disease, the force of 5,900 that had faced off against the American forces in September of 1777 at Saratoga was reduced to 4,200 in captivity at Cambridge by the following fall.

As suggested by the description of life in the rudimentary barracks at Cambridge, conditions there for the captives were brutal, but the worst was yet to come. In November of 1778, they were sent to march overland all the way to Virginia, over 700 miles (1,100 kilometers) through weather that turned vicious by the time they arrived in Charlottesville, where they would stay for nearly two years.

There, they found even worse shelter available than there had been in Cambridge, and many of them initially took to camping in the woods, as it was more comfortable than conditions in the makeshift barracks. Rations were at times reduced to nothing more than cornmeal, and the pace of desertions increased. Some deserters, like Arthur, became involved with and married local women, fading into the countryside as new Americans, but many planned to find their ways back into service with the British army.

They were moved again in the fall of 1780, as British forces approached their encampment in Virginia, forced to march again, this time to Maryland. Only about 2,650 remained by this time. The following May, they were moved to Pennsylvania, where they were eventually settled in Lancaster. That September, their officers were sent to Connecticut, and in October, Cornwallis surrendered at Yorktown (as seen in *The Siege*).

The remaining prisoners of war from the first major British defeat were finally freed by the Congress' ratification of the peace treaty in April of 1783. After over five and a half years of captivity and well over a thousand miles (1,600 kilometers) of hard marching, fewer than a thousand British soldiers remained when they were eventually released to find their way home to England.

The treatment of British prisoners of war may seem shocking to our modern sensibilities. Indeed, it was downright gentle in comparison to the horrors endured by Americans who were taken prisoner during the Revolution. As alluded to here, the Parliament did not legally recognize the rebellious colonials as a legitimate military force, and so even the normal customs of war were not held to be due to them.

Many American soldiers and militiamen who were captured by the British were packed onto prison hulks — dismasted and stripped ships — in the harbors of New-York and other ports along the East Coast. There, many of them died of disease and starvation, making it more akin to a death sentence than to mere imprisonment for crimes against the Crown. The recent novel *The Turncoat's Widow*, by Mally Becker, gives a harrowing view of life — and death — aboard the prison hulks of New-York.

Today, of course, the Geneva Convention governs the treatment of prisoners taken during wars (among other martial matters). Of course, not all nations are signatories, not all armed forces even represent nations, and not all those taken captive in armed conflicts between nations are recognized as legitimate prisoners of war . . . so mistreatment of military men and women taken captive continues to the present day, to various degrees of severity.

Writing from the perspective of a British soldier sent to suppress an illegitimate insurrection was an interesting exercise, but it was made more natural by a visit to the United Kingdom a few months before I set out to start writing this book. Hadrian's Wall, which Arthur described being used as an impromptu quarry by locals over the ages, made a deep impression on me, and the windswept rolling hills of that region were simply glorious to experience.

Of course, the wall is strictly protected today, and a number of really wonderful sites help visitors gain a sense of connection to a thousand years and more of history that's unfolded on that terrain.

Acknowledgements

Writing from the "other side" of a conflict so inherently one-sided in our national mythos is a challenging undertaking, and I am exceptionally grateful for the careful records preserved by the British and German officers who led the Convention Army into its ordeal.

In addition, Thomas Fleming's richly-detailed article "Gentleman Johnny's Wandering Army," from the December 1972 volume of *American Heritage* magazine was an invaluable source, and is well worth reading for deeper understanding of these events.

That those records are available with relative ease is thanks to the work done by Google Books, the Library of Congress, and others, who have undertaken the complex and painstaking task of converting fragile paper documents into indexed and searchable electronic records.

Once again, my editor, Jen McDonnell, helped me to ensure that this story made as much sense as possible. After I realized that the initial draft needed substantial re-working, she helped me to ensure that the changes hadn't come at the cost of continuity.

The story is more internally consistent and a far smoother read for her input, and I am glad to acknowledge her assistance. Any errors I introduced after her edits are wholly my own fault, of course.

Thank You

I deeply appreciate you spending the past couple of hundred pages with the characters and events of a world long past, yet hopefully relevant today.

If you enjoyed this book, I'd also be grateful for a kind review on your favorite bookseller's Web site or social media outlet. Word of mouth is the best way to make me successful, so that I can bring you even more high-quality stories of bygone times.

To hear about my newest releases, appearances, special offers, and more, sign up for my monthly newsletter at https://bit.ly/HedborNewsletter.

I'd love to hear directly from you, too — feel free to reach out to me via my Facebook page, Twitter feed, or Web site and let me know what you liked, and what you would like me to work on more.

Again, thank you for reading, for telling your friends about this book, for giving it as a gift or dropping off a copy in your favorite classroom or library. With your support and encouragement, we'll find even more times and places to explore together.

larsdhhedbor.com
Facebook: Lars.D.H.Hedbor
@LarsDHHedbor on Twitter

Made in the USA
Columbia, SC
29 October 2022